"Kendrick does n...

Graham pulled Linnet ...ap, displacing more of her skirts until half her thighs were exposed to the muted daylight and gentle breeze. "I think I should have you instead."

Linnet lifted her gaze to meet his and found his expression fierce. Possessive. Just now she could only care that he was a man.

And she, for her part, remained one aching woman who had been too long deprived.

Graham might leave her tomorrow, or he could simply vanish from her life as startlingly as he had entered it. She'd be a folly-fallen fool to allow this moment with him to pass through her fingers.

Linnet had only one condition and she whispered it in his ear.

"Show me everything...."

Blaze™

Dear Reader,

I can't say how thrilled I am to present my first-ever time travel story that combines two of my favorite genres— a sexy Harlequin Blaze story and a medieval historical. Those of you who've checked out my Harlequin Historical books know how much I love the Middle Ages, so it was a real treat to bring that lush setting into the pages of a red-hot Blaze read. And since one of my ongoing themes as a historical writer is a personal conviction that women were strong and resourceful in any era, it has been really gratifying to pair up my contemporary hero with a medieval maiden who proves a more than worthy partner.

But of course, in fiction, half the fun is getting there. I'll let you see how Graham and Linnet match hearts and wits in *Hidden Obsession*, and I hope you'll join me in watching the PERFECT TIMING miniseries develop next month with another exciting story, *Highland Fling* by Jennifer LaBrecque.

Happy reading,

Joanne Rock

HIDDEN OBSESSION

Joanne Rock

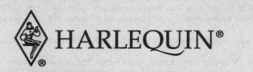

HARLEQUIN®

TORONTO • NEW YORK • LONDON
AMSTERDAM • PARIS • SYDNEY • HAMBURG
STOCKHOLM • ATHENS • TOKYO • MILAN • MADRID
PRAGUE • WARSAW • BUDAPEST • AUCKLAND

ISBN 0-373-79260-3

HIDDEN OBSESSION

This edition published by arrangement with Harlequin Books S.A.

® and TM are trademarks of the publisher. Trademarks indicated with
® are registered in the United States Patent and Trademark Office, the
Canadian Trade Marks Office and in other countries.

www.eHarlequin.com

Printed in U.S.A.

ABOUT THE AUTHOR

Joanne Rock traces her passion for all things medieval from the Arthurian tradition to John Keats's "The Eve of St. Agnes" and Heath Ledger in *A Knight's Tale*. She knew she wanted to try her hand at a medieval story after Elizabeth Lowell's *Forbidden* kept her enthralled through a seven-hour layover in Newark, figuring any tale that could make an extended airport stint fun was nothing short of brilliant. Today, Joanne indulges her love of sexy contemporary romance as well as her medieval appreciation in her stories for Harlequin Blaze, Signature Select and Harlequin Historical. A writer who adores new challenges, Joanne leaped at the chance to try something new in a time travel book. Visit Joanne at www.JoanneRock.com to enter monthly contests and learn more about her work.

Books by Joanne Rock

For Winnie Griggs, Tanya Michaels, Anna DeStefano, Dianna Love Snell and Annie Oortman, thank you for giving me a break from this book to visit with you at Moonlight & Magnolias so I could come home recharged and excited to finish Graham and Linnet's story. Tanya and Anna, what would I do without the bonus margaritas you send my way? Winnie, thanks for reading for me and cheering on my Muse from Day One. And for Dianna and Annie, thank you for always having time to talk books with me! You all make this work so much fun.

And for the talented sister of my heart, Catherine Mann, who knows what I'm trying to accomplish even when I can't remember. Thank you for sharing your brilliant insights with me and inspiring me to be the best I can be. I adore you, dear friend!

_1_

IF THERE HAD BEEN EVEN a hint of cosmic order in the universe, Graham Lawson wouldn't have had to show up on a Hollywood set for the rest of his life.

Wrenching his practice sword out of A-list actor Brendan Jameson's hands before the guy could spend another moment checking out his teeth in the polished reflection, Los Angeles Police Department weapons expert Graham stuffed the blade in its sheath before folding the antique piece in a length of cloth for transport back to his private collection. He couldn't afford another day away from his current investigation with a new brand of flesh-peddling gangbangers running around L.A. and keeping his department hopping. Especially since this latest crew of felons had demonstrated a preference for medieval weaponry to inflict twisted sex pain on their victims. They showed a hell of a lot more facility with their arms than pretty-boy Brendan at Graham's sideline as a weapons consultant for an action-adventure flick.

"See you tomorrow, coach?" Brendan asked, sipping his Evian between bouts of the makeup artist's brush while he prepped for his close-ups in studio 3A.

"I don't know. I think the director said something about shooting the remaining scenes with a copied sword." Graham zipped the leather satchel he'd used for transporting an assortment of weapons to and from the set for the past two months. The gig had started out as a favor to his ex-girlfriend, a bit-part actress in the film they were shooting and a woman who'd barely waited for Graham to finish his first sword-wielding lesson with the starring actor before she'd thrown herself at Brendan. Currently she stood by the refreshment table, leaning over to push her boobs up for more cleavage.

Nice. The kicker of it all was that Graham had made a three-thousand-mile relocation from the NYPD to the LAPD in order to be with the woman he'd met while providing extra security to a Manhattan set where she'd had a role in a music video. Good thing he liked the weather out here or he might just have been pissed off at her.

"But what about the choreography of the fight sequences?" Brendan held up a hand to pause the makeup artist in mid sweep of her brush full of bronzer.

Graham couldn't resent the guy—too much—since Brendan was clueless about Graham's ex-girlfriend's maneuvering.

"You're looking more at ease every day," Graham fibbed for the greater good. But then, Graham would never be able to think about dividing up action sequences into smaller vignettes to best show off his abs, either. In a world that emphasized how something looked over actual accomplishment though, maybe Brendan had an advantage.

Welcome to Hollywood.

"Killer." Brendan flashed a thumbs-up sign, tipping off both Graham and his makeup artist that the conversation was over.

Graham's phone started ringing the moment he finished packing his gear. He answered as he wound his way through the cavernous soundstage toward the studio back lot, his vintage sword secured across his back in a custom-made carrying case.

"Lawson." Blinking against the bright afternoon sun that seemed to shine non-stop to the eyes of an east-coast transplant, Graham bummed a ride to the parking lot off a gopher speeding by in a golf cart.

Another thing he couldn't get used to about this city, you had to drive everywhere.

"It's Miguel. You done playing Gene Kelly yet?"

Graham's twenty-five-year-old partner had laughed his ass off at the idea of Brendan Jameson cutting Graham's action sequence into choreography snippets so he could remember them better.

"I'm getting in the truck now." Graham floated the golf-cart-driving kid a few bucks for his trouble and loaded the satchel into the front seat of his Sierra Denali pickup—a kick-ass ride he refused to trade even though it guzzled fuel like there was no tomorrow.

Besides, the truck had proved more loyal than most of the women in his life and that ought to count for something.

"You in the mood to maintain your highbrow commitment to the arts?"

"What's that supposed to mean?"

"There's some kind of art exhibit in town called Sex Through the Ages, and our guys found a flyer for the thing in a search of a Guardian member's glove compartment this morning."

The gang calling themselves the Guardians had upped the stakes two weeks ago when they had begun kidnapping area women for participation in twisted, occasionally brutal, sex rituals as a form of hazing for their new members. Leads were scarce other than a few instances of weaponry with medieval flare. Maces. Scythes. Or so went the rumors. No old-school weapons had been confiscated, but in a couple of police reports, witnesses claimed to have seen the tools. Then two women who'd escaped the Guardians had come home with scythes tattooed on their thighs and tales of lurid and sometimes sadistic sex rites carried out with cultist attention to detail.

Cops all over the city had moved the case up to their first priority.

"Sex Through the Ages?" Graham pulled out of the studio lot and headed north toward the interstate. "Sounds like a docudrama on pornography. How is that an art exhibit?"

"Beats me. The brochure shows some naked paintings and a kinky costume display, but I figured you'd want to take a look at the medieval section since our guys seem to dig the Crusader tie-in."

"Right. Where is this place?" Graham didn't mind the fieldwork since—aside from his crappy sideline as a weapons consultant on the movie—he spent most of his time behind a desk these days. His expertise had propelled him through the police ranks with gratifying speed, but there came a point where he missed the time in the field that made the job real. Intense.

"The show is at the Getty Center. There's an exit for it off the 405." Miguel started rattling off directions but Graham could picture the place. "It closes at six, though. You'd better step on it."

"Crap. That was the most important part of this conversation, bud. You're supposed to lead with the big news and work your way down through the rest." Graham leaned on the accelerator and hit the passing lane more aggressively since his dashboard clock read 5:40.

"Then you're really not going to like this." Miguel cleared his throat and lowered his voice. "Eyewitness reports from the UCLA campus say the Guardians took two other women from a summer workshop in parapsychology this morning. One of the witnesses got a good look at a weapon they were carrying and I'm going to send it over to you now. It sounded like a scythe when she first described it, but the artist's picture shows something more unusual."

"I'm on it." Graham processed the information as he flew down the highway, the smoggy breeze whipping through the open window of his truck not doing jack to clear his head.

He didn't know where a bunch of twenty-year-old street thugs were finding the kinds of weapons that few collectors could get their hands on, but obviously the

Guardian organization was a hell of a lot more sophisticated than he'd first realized.

Which made them a whole lot more dangerous. And even harder to catch. Graham was pretty damn certain this group wasn't visiting museums in their spare time for inspiration on their sick rituals, but maybe these guys were pulling research from some B-movie version of battles in the Middle Ages and the helpless role of the village wenches. He'd have to remember to speak to the department's psych guys about the tight brotherhood mentality of the gang. They might be able to profile their ringleaders a little more narrowly if the Guardians were really grooving on the pseudo-historical roots of their crime ring.

Eighteen minutes later, Graham jogged into the J. Paul Getty Museum with the valuable historic sword strapped on his back in its protective case. He hadn't planned to make a stop on the way home and he couldn't afford to leave a ten-thousand-dollar weapon unguarded. Now he flashed his badge enough times to warrant the appearance of a management type who understood the need for speed and discretion. After giving the okay to keep the museum open later on a private basis just for the evening, the museum's assistant director called out a night watchman to show Graham around the Sex Through the Ages exhibit.

Progress.

The old guy was quiet, which suited Graham fine as he scanned room after room in search of anything that might clue him in to Guardian rituals or shed light on the meaning of the scythe. The drawing Miguel had e-mailed him had been an oddly shaped halberd with a curved hilt. Similar to a poleax, a halberd could be used as both a dagger and an ax, but the slight arc in the haft was a twist Graham had never come across before. He'd also never seen the style of engraving on the handle, which looked too distinct to mark the piece as an antique, although that might be an exaggeration by the artist to capture details the eyewitness had described.

Knowing the Sex Through the Ages exhibit was probably not the place to find clues about the weapon anyhow, Graham tucked away the PDA with the picture and concentrated on the task at hand. For all he knew, the traveling museum show had been just a matter of curiosity to the suspect who'd had a flyer about it. Graham needed to be open to other leads that didn't have anything to do with weaponry.

One of the echoing museum halls displayed a history of dildos. Another showcased the development of undergarments meant to tantalize. There was a sprawling section dedicated to porn, but those specialty exhibits were sandwiched between bigger rooms dedicated to various time periods.

Boot soles squeaking on the polished museum floor, Graham made tracks for the Middle Ages area that had been draped with crushed red velvet curtains tied back with golden cord.

Music had been piped in that Graham could only assume was period accurate. The sound of monks chanting a cappella provided an interesting accompa-

niment to racy displays ranging from provocative paintings to drawings of sexual enhancement aids and a
PowerPoint projection on a blank wall depicting various
methods of medieval birth control, all of which looked
fairly revolting.

Why would any of this be interesting to the Guardians? Was there a clue to their sex rites contained in the
ten-minute narrated slide show about the subversive
sexuality of witch hunts? Would their group care that
medieval society blatantly encouraged sex outside
marriage in the subtly written code of chivalry?

"Damn." Graham muttered under his breath, resent-
ing the lost time here if the museum lead turned out to
be a dead end.

"Perhaps you would like to see the collection of
paintings, sir?" the night watchman asked from a few
feet behind. "Some were painted within the time period
and others were crafted afterward yet still reflect the
medieval sentiment."

Nodding, Graham shifted the position of the sword
sheath on his back and followed the guy past a glass
display case of supposed chastity belts along with a
disclaimer about the authenticity of the items, which
many believed a myth. As they reached the wall of
paintings, Graham realized the collection resembled
nothing he'd ever seen at an art gallery.

Not that he spent much time in museums, but he
seemed to recall the general rule of hanging visual art
was to give each piece enough white space to appreciate the works individually. Here, the canvases had been

hung close together with disparate themes clashing up against one another. The rougher, two-dimensional style of period pieces butted up against soft-focus Victorian interpretations of the Middle Ages.

Graham could scarcely take it all in, other than an overall impression of numerous curvy maidens falling out of their clothes. Knights and peasants, kings and nobles filled out the periphery of the presentation, their swords brandishing at every angle like a field of strutting lovers flexing their he-man prowess in an age-old mating call.

"Do you have any questions I can help you with, sir?" the old night watchman asked in his gravelly voice, hands clasped behind his back.

"Not yet." Graham didn't know what he was looking for here, but somehow this section of paintings gave him the sense that he'd come closer. Shifting his gaze downward from the sweep of images across the wall, he spotted a weapon similar to the photo Miguel had sent.

A halberd with a slightly curved haft, although the piece bore none of the peculiar chain-link-style markings witnesses claimed to have seen on the Guardians' weapon on the UCLA campus.

Moving closer to inspect the canvas, he squinted into the dark shadows of the artwork but couldn't make out any more detail. The blade rested at ease against a hay bale while a knight on the other side of the image removed his helm to rest at the side of a country road.

"I don't get it." Graham stood back from the painting

again to see if he'd missed something. "How does this picture show anything about sex? Why include something as innocuous as a knight catching a few Zs as part of the exhibit?"

The answers were probably here somewhere on one of the zillion little placards for patrons who wanted a self-guided tour of the show, but Graham didn't have a lot of time for research with two more women now in the Guardians' hands.

The watchman stepped closer, blue eyes keen, as if he'd been eager for an opportunity to share what he knew. The guy probably didn't get the chance to talk to many people if his shift started at six and the museum closed early three nights a week.

"The growing church frowned on the sexual practices of societies with ancient pagan roots, so we don't have many records of private life from this time period since works of a corporeal nature were often burned or destroyed in the name of protecting the public."

"Censorship has been around a while." Gritting his teeth against his impatience, Graham stuffed his hands in his pockets and waited for more.

"Because of revisionist-style censorship, most of our remaining historical evidence is subversive and hints at a society that reveled in its sexuality even as it worked hard to keep their intimate practices behind closed doors."

"Okay." Graham paced around another case containing polished wooden dildos. *Wooden?* "And my apologies for seeming dense, but I still don't understand any hidden agenda for the knight resting his tired ass at the end of a long tournament day."

"Perfectly understandable." The guard adjusted his navy-blue cap over wild gray hair escaping at all angles. "And we hope that reinforces our need for placing the paintings in strategic juxtaposition, to evoke the way medieval audiences would have viewed the work. You see how the knight setting aside his arms and making himself comfortable is right beside *Madeline After Prayer* in which a young woman undresses for bed?"

Graham looked to the left at a richly detailed depiction of a woman sliding pearls from her hair, her clothes slipping off her shoulders.

"Well, the story behind the painting is that the woman has said a prayer to dream of the man she will marry and her lover has hidden himself in her closet that night to make certain it is *he* who appears in her thoughts, since he plans to steal into bed with her after watching her undress." The guard gave a sly smile. "The knight in the other painting hints at the unseen man hidden in this image, waiting within Madeline's wardrobe."

"I see." Finally. Although Graham sure as hell hoped the Guardians left more overt messages in their chain of crimes. "Can you tell me anything about this weapon?"

Pointing to the halberd, he dragged his eyes off buxom young Madeline, an interesting combination of prayerful innocent and lush temptress. Not that Graham was here to gawk at women trapped in old canvas.

"Perhaps, but if I may just point out one more thing you might be interested in here...."

Graham followed the watchman's finger as he pointed toward some of the details at the edge of Madeline's image. He leaned in closer to look and then—

Wham!

The guard shoved him forward with surprising force, propelling him toward the painting. But instead of crashing into the wall of glass that protected all the artwork, Graham found himself hurtling forward through endless darkness until his mind slipped into an even blacker fog than the void through which he traveled.

LINNET WELBORNE KICKED OFF her slipper with a thrust of one foot, sending the delicate velvet shoe hurtling into the wall on the other side of her bed, where it crashed and fell to the floor with a soft thud.

Ripping off her other slipper, she shot it like an arrow from her fingertips, hitting her lyre with bull's-eye accuracy and calling forth a discordant twang of the strings. She silently damned both velvet articles along with every other item of clothing her flap-mouthed, onion-eyed, fly-bitten betrothed had given her.

She would have never worn a stitch of it if not for her beslubbering stepbrothers' insistence this eve.

"May I help you, my lady?" her maid called to her from the door, no doubt dismayed to find herself locked out of Linnet's chamber for the night. But it served Edana right. Linnet had once been attended by a beloved nurse she'd known since childhood, but these days, her maid was the snippy little sister of the monster Linnet would one day wed.

And "one day" seemed to be approaching too swiftly if reports of her betrothed's return to England could be trusted.

"No, thank you, Edana. I'm sure it will please you to be excused from my company this eve since you find it so loathsome." Linnet knew she couldn't lock out the spiteful wench the whole night since all her belongings were in here, but she could not allow the woman's barbs to spew forth unchecked, either.

"Do you think it wise to anger me, Linnet?" Edana's words were no less sharp for the barrier of the oak door they passed through, all pretense of servitude vanished in an honest moment, since Edana had never felt one bit inclined to *serve* anyone but herself.

"Perhaps you should ask yourself if you think it wise to anger *me,* Edana, since I am to have the ear of your brother when he returns from war." God help her. "I think you will find him more kindly disposed to his wife's wishes than you suspect."

She lied as smoothly as her morals would allow— which was actually a good deal—but Edana's only response was a high bark of laughter before she retreated down the corridor away from Linnet's door. At least Edana didn't try to pretend that Linnet's marriage would be a peaceful union the way her brothers did. All three of the elder Welborne males insisted Burke Kendrick would be a good husband to her because of his strength and might, or perhaps because of his wealth and prominence.

But Linnet knew Kendrick's mercilessness had

brought him his coin along with the knights who swore fealty to him. Her stepbrothers had been easily persuaded to part with her when Kendrick had flashed a bit of gold beneath their noses and the promise of new lands.

For their greed, Linnet would one day have to answer to the most brutal man in all of England. And no doubt, she'd have to answer to his insufferable sister as well.

Fumbling with the laces of her gown, Linnet yanked on the ties until she'd freed enough room to step out of her surcoat, another costly gift from her betrothed.

A beautiful body deserves to be beautifully displayed.

Kendrick's words echoed in her memory, his dark stare unnerving her that day he'd delivered trunk after trunk of new garments more worthy of her. Ha! The man had looked at her as if he'd prefer to see her naked and her stepbrothers had done naught to stop his roving hands. They'd been too busy estimating the cost of the early wedding gifts.

Now, clad in her own undergarments as she readied the chamber for bed, Linnet prayed she would not be visited by more dream visions of her future with him. Nay, she'd rather escape into the more fanciful visions she'd been having lately—images filled with wanton encounters involving a strange man she'd never seen.

Foolishness, surely. But far more pleasant than her real life. She swallowed the burning sensation in the back of her throat at the idea of marriage to a man rumored to have an insatiable appetite for virgins in his bed. Half the serving women at Kendrick Keep had been initiated by him. Even Edana admitted as much.

So, Linnet wondered as she pulled back the bed linens, how would the brute maintain interest in a marriage that would provide him with a virgin only one night?

She did not care about his interest half so much as she cared about protecting her legitimate children from the avarice of a proliferation of her husband's bastards. She would run anywhere from this marriage—gladly forsake every stupid velvet slipper and golden bauble for her freedom. But Kendrick and her stepbrothers had taken pains to ensure her isolation at her eldest brother's stronghold on the southern coast.

Escape was impossible.

Pulling the strands of smooth pearls from her hair, Linnet was about to slide beneath her sheets when a rustling noise sounded on the far side of her room. Surely she was full of foolish fancy after brooding about Kendrick, but she could not help the peculiar notion that a man's eyes followed her once again.

2

IF GRAHAM WAS DREAMING, he'd rather not wake up just now.

As it was, he cursed himself for the small movement of his foot that halted the gorgeous fantasy female from taking off the rest of her clothes. She stood motionless for a long moment before charging toward the closet where he seemed to hide out of her view. He watched her through a cutout in the wood, a design emblem carved out at eye level.

The dream made perfect sense for the most part since he'd handily inserted himself right into the same voyeuristic situation as the unseen knight hidden in a wardrobe suggested by the museum painting. The bed, the loom at the foot of bed, the woman slipping out of her clothes—it was all here. Graham just wished he could connect how he'd gone from looking at an art exhibit to dreaming about it. Shouldn't he be on duty right now? Damned if he could recall what he'd done on his shift after leaving the Getty Center. For that matter, his brain couldn't seem to dredge up a memory of ever leaving the museum.

"You cursed lazy cat." The voluptuous vision squawked at a mangy black feline curled at the foot of her bed before plucking the thing off the covers and tossing it unceremoniously toward the closet. "I don't keep you for your stingy company, you know. I expect you to at least keep my chamber free of rodents, do you hear?"

The scruffy beast stretched long and then arched high, indifferent to the request. After peering about lazily, it took up a new position on its haunches, where it proceeded to lick one paw to swipe repeatedly over an ear.

"Oh. Now that's impressive." The curvy blonde stomped closer and, although the tops of her breasts jiggled enticingly with the movement, Graham thought the dream seemed a bit too tame. His imagination usually generated more graphic scenarios, although he had to admit this lady's unassisted jiggle beat the hell out of anything his ex had ever managed with a push-up bra.

Perhaps if he woke himself and then fell back to sleep, he'd have better luck next time because he was more than ready to see the medieval maiden in an X-rated fairy tale. He pinched himself hard on the arm.

Damn. That hurt.

His arm stung and he was still staring at the blonde through the cutout shape of an equal-armed cross. A Crusader's cross. The woman barreled closer, clearly angry at her cat and determined the animal should investigate the wardrobe where Graham stood. Why couldn't he wake up and what the hell had happened at the Getty Center that he couldn't remember anything after the guard had…pushed him?

"Honestly, Sebastian, you are the most worthless creature to ever—" Her words halted as she swung open the door to the wardrobe and stood face-to-face with Graham.

The perfect time for him to wake up. Only he still stood there, staring at her waist-length hair, smelling her clean, simple scent. He reached to touch her, ready to insert himself into the fantasy—so to speak—but the woman jumped back with a squeal, dropping the cat as she clamped a hand over her own mouth.

The fear in her eyes rocked him. That kind of emotion was no illusion. The encounter bore no resemblance to any dream he'd ever had.

"Scared you, did I?" Graham lifted his empty hands to assure her he was unarmed. "Sorry about that. I'm not sure how I ended up in there— That is—"

"How did you get in here?" She removed her hand from her mouth, just far away enough to give her space to talk without opening up much potential for screaming.

He'd really freaked her out. And she was beginning to do the same for him.

Before he could answer her question, the woman dove for a small chest beside the wardrobe and came up holding a dagger. Her long hair swirled around her shoulders with the rapid movement, her ample chest heaving with the effort, but by now Graham could no longer enjoy the view. He was too stunned that he hadn't been dreaming.

"Answer me." The woman spoke softly as she backed away from him, her dagger gripped expertly in one hand while she extended her other for balance.

"You could whip the pants off Brendan Jameson."

Her technique was freaking perfect. Too bad she looked so serious about castrating him or Graham might have been able to appreciate all the finer points of her stance.

God, he had to get his head out of dream mode and figure out what the hell had happened. Where was he?

"What?" She snatched up her discarded dress in a moment of modesty and blew her battle-ready pose to fling fabric around herself.

Amateur move.

"Never mind. I was wrong."

He lunged in on his toes for the knife, knowing she would never be able to manage much footwork with the slippery, satiny stuff of her gown to trip her up. He squeezed her wrist just hard enough to force the release of the blade, but he hadn't counted on a blow to the back of his head from her fist, her hand knocking aside the sword case he still wore strapped to his back.

A string of curses ripped from his lips but, to his utter amazement, his sparring partner clamped her soft white hand—the same damn one she'd just clubbed him with—over his mouth to silence him.

"Do you want to call forth every man-at-arms in the keep?" Her clipped accent wasn't quite British and it wasn't quite French, but something in between that Graham couldn't identify.

Where the hell was he?

For one long moment, they knelt on the floor together, close enough to kiss but locked in struggle, and took each other's measure. Graham became aware of each delicate fingertip cradling his cheek, the wild pulse of her body thumping through her hand just exactly where his lips touched her palm. Her skin smelled like roses. And for some dumb-ass reason, he decided to lick her to see what she tasted like.

She flinched as if burned.

"Do not—" She swiped her hand across her white…under-dress, for lack of a better word. Her gown had fallen to the floor again, forgotten in the struggle for her dagger, which now resided safely in the waist of his jeans. "Do not ever do that."

"What do you care if I call forth the whole castle, eh, damsel?" Graham couldn't even believe he was having this conversation with a woman he didn't know in a room he'd never seen, and—if she could be believed— in a medieval stronghold?

Curious now, he rose to his feet and left her there on the floor to wriggle back into her clothes, since it seemed important to her to put the overdress on top of the under-dress. A damn lot of clothes. He hadn't even copped much of a feel in the tussle for the knife thanks to all the layers of skirts and whatnot.

Definitely a shame.

Striding across the room to a high, narrow window, Graham peered out and half expected to see a Holly-wood back lot or a darkened studio full of props and cameras. Instead, rolling green countryside spanned out as far as he could see. The scent of the ocean rode the wind on a warm summer breeze and he guessed the sea must be on the other side of the building. Too bad the richly dark soil and closely packed deciduous trees in the distance didn't look much like the California coast.

And…holy crap. The sun was setting on the wrong side, placing the body of water to the south instead of the west where it damn well should have been.

"Where the hell am I?" He turned to the blond beauty wiggling into her clothes, her hips swaying in a hurried dance. "And who the hell are you?"

"Vile beast." She crossed her arms and presented him with a snooty look. "How dare you speak to me so foully in my chamber, in my home, as if you hadn't been just gawking at my nakedness like a slag-bellied swine."

Graham ran a hand over his gut, half-scared what he'd find since his whole reality had shifted.

"No slag here, lady. And if you think that white dress thing you're wearing passes for nakedness, you must not have seen any beer commercials lately." He offered her his hand. "I'm Graham Lawson, LAPD."

She stared at his hand with obvious disgust for all of two seconds before she busied herself with more gown straightening and smoothing so she wouldn't have to touch him. What a piece of work.

"Linnet of Welborne, as I'm sure you well know. This LAPD is your title?"

"Feeling sort of rumpled with two dresses on, aren't you?" He stared meaningfully at her restless fingers and dropped his hand to his side. "I'm with local law enforcement, but I'm a little cloudy about how I got here. You say you never saw me come into your chamber?"

Something wasn't adding up and he hated that he saw no sign of the museum guard, the painting he'd been studying or any of the other Sex Through the Ages exhibits.

"I would never remove my garments in a man's presence. I had no idea you were hiding in the wardrobe."

The tone of her strange accent echoed in his ear with unnerving implications. When combined with other evidence like the stone walls of the room, the richly detailed tapestries, the exotic clothing this Linnet of Welborne wore and the view outside her window, Graham upgraded unnerving to unsettling as hell. He had a case to investigate and he couldn't afford any practical jokes costing him valuable time.

"Why don't we just assume that I hit my head and don't have a clue how I got here? Can you tell me where we are right now and—um—that is…what time period you're showcasing with the dress-up clothes?"

"Of all the folly-fallen, rump-fed foolishness—"

"Can we cut the complaints and get to the information, please?"

"You are in the private living quarters of Welborne Keep in the year of our Lord 1190. Pray, do not let me delay you if you wish to be on your way."

Holy—

Either he'd fallen and hit his head hard enough to put himself in the craziest coma ever, or this Linnet was an incredible actress with an unlimited prop budget on her hands.

Either of which were about as likely as the other stupid scenario that kept insinuating itself in Graham's head.

The old night watchman had shoved Graham right into that medieval painting and somehow propelled him backward in time over eight hundred years.

However he looked at it, this was turning out to be a hell of a day. Deciding he'd just play it out until he could get a better handle on what was happening to him, he figured he'd explore the surroundings and interrogate Linnet until he found out what kind of game she played. With any luck, she was simply part of some bizarre living exhibit that was some crazy creative type's idea of art. For now, Graham's cop brain zeroed in on the one continuity item that didn't make sense if Linnet of Welborne was really some long-ago medieval lady.

"If my shouting would have brought a slew of protectors running to your rescue a few minutes ago, why would you ever want me to be quiet?"

THERE WAS A *MAN* in Linnet's chamber.

A big, attractive, dangerous man wearing foreign clothes who spoke with an accent she could not place. This same man had watched in silence as she'd removed her surcoat, and he'd flicked his tongue along her palm in a gesture that should have been obscene, yet her skin still burned from the contact.

Her betrothed would kill her if he found out about this.

For that matter, Graham Lawson LAPD could kill her at any moment. Or abduct her. Or abuse her. And yet, he had not threatened her. Had not turned her weapon against her or lifted the formidable sword he carried to otherwise frighten her. Already those simple clues told her his character ranked above Kendrick's. Not that it said much for the stranger, considering the depth of her loathing for Kendrick.

Swallowing her fears, she clasped her hands behind her back to hide their nervous twitching.

"I attempted to spare your life with my warning. But if you do not wish a chance to escape quietly, by all means let us make enough noise to alert my step-brothers to your presence."

His gaze narrowed, his silvery-blue eyes locked on her. No bulky chain mail hid his form. The striped shirt he wore fastened neatly up the front, the cut flattering to his straight shoulders even if the shape of the garment resembled none she'd ever seen. He wore his sword strapped to his back in an unusual sheath. His braies— or whatever the garment that covered his legs—fit him so admirably she could not quite convince herself that it was the blue fabric that drew her eye.

Wrenching her gaze back up to his face, she studied his visage with equal interest. No facial hair hid his features, but a dark shadow of whiskers covered his jaw. Raven-colored hair had been trimmed close to his head, accentuating his unusual eyes and stark features too strong to be handsome.

Intriguing, perhaps. Compelling, even.

So much so that for a moment, she half wondered if this could be the mysterious stranger who'd come to her in her dreams lately. Her body heated at the thought.

She'd told herself she had merely begun to experience sensual dreams because of her prolonged virginity, thanks to her family keeping her under lock and key to honor her betrothal. Plus she'd caught one of the knights swiving a maid behind the kitchens a fortnight ago. A sight that had made her quite…restless…ever since.

"I find it hard to believe you would be concerned about sparing the life of a stranger who spied on you. What's in it for you?"

She blinked, grateful for the change of subject since she could not afford to lose herself in sensual visions while a stranger remained in her chamber. She puzzled over his odd turn of phrase even though she suspected she understood the meaning.

"You mean to ask how my silence benefits me?" She saw no harm in telling him a portion of the truth. "I am not particularly fond of my stepbrothers and I fear any disruption to their evening of drinking and whoring will not be appreciated, but make no mistake, their displeasure is far less intimidating than a man who wishes me bodily harm."

"Harm?" His head cocked back as if surprised. "I don't know what angle you're playing, lady, but maybe I'd better step out into the hallway or at least open the door so you can't cry harassment at a later date. I don't know how I got in the wardrobe thing over there, but I sure as hell didn't come in here with the intent to hurt you."

"Only to watch me without my knowledge." Her skin tingled with awareness at the memory of how much she'd disrobed under his watchful eyes.

"Again, not my intention, but the view seemed too fortuitous to just close my eyes and ignore the show." He surprised her with a tight pull of his lips that just might have been a smile. "Some women would be flattered."

"I find that highly unlikely." She thought her skin had flushed before? Now the heat crawled right out of her bodice to climb her neck and heat her cheeks. The man spoke with far too much familiarity. And that strange accent—she could not come close to guessing the land of his birth. "In fact, I find your whole story implausible."

"You want to talk about implausible? Believe me, sweetheart, I've got a doozy for you but I don't think you're in any shape to listen with an open mind." He pulled her dagger from his waist and set it aside. Out of her reach on the trunk at the end of her bed. "I'd rather not risk another go-round with a knife. Not hiding any more blades in all those clothes, are you?"

She thought to question him about the nature of a *doozy* and then stopped herself since it didn't matter.

"I do not think that I will divulge my secrets to you, intruder." She did not care for his tone or his manner, even if he didn't seem interested in abducting her or abusing her. "And since you say you do not know how you came to be in my chamber, I realize you cannot serve any useful purpose for me. Perhaps we have reached an impasse and I will call for my pig-witted kin after all."

She moved toward her door but he reached to restrain her movement. He gripped her arm firmly but not hard enough to leave bruises. She spared a glance down at his hand and was surprised at the cleanliness of his skin, so unlike her stepbrothers or Kendrick, who were convinced that bathing made them more susceptible to illness.

Sweet, merciful heaven, this man even smelled clean.

"Don't." His word was more fierce than his hold. "Wait."

She sucked in a breath, praying she had not misjudged his character. Praying she would not embarrass herself by falling against this intriguing stranger and begging him to take her away from here. Anywhere.

"Be honest. Why are you so interested in how I got into the room?"

The low timbre of his voice suggested intimacy. Confidences. The tone sent a shiver of awareness through a body suddenly tingling with anticipation. She swallowed back the unexpected flicker of heat and sought the right words that would convey her situation without arousing his sympathy for her brothers.

Her betrothed.

If Graham Lawson could be bought with gold, she would be better off not revealing the identity of her powerful future husband. Still, she could not overlook the opportunity he presented.

"I am not so much interested in how you arrived in the chamber as how you arrived in the keep."

"Why?" He looked over his shoulder toward the arrow slit where he had peered out before, but still he did not release her.

What did he seek out her window? Did he search for an enemy?

"Because if I knew how you slipped into the walls, I would use that same way to sneak out." Her heartbeat jumped oddly at his touch while the heat of his hand penetrated the sleeve of her kirtle. A friendly gesture, not one of restraint. The difference was obvious.

Delicious.

"Whether I remember the way in or not, I assure you, I can get us out." He released her arm, his words certain and laced with endless male confidence.

Linnet found herself mourning the loss of his touch.

"Is that so?" She thought about her brothers keeping watch in the courtyard and did not believe Graham. Yet she wanted to. Desperately.

"Lady, I need to get the hell out of here ASAP."

"Excuse me?" His unusual speech combined with his apparent affection for reeling off letters made him difficult to understand.

"I said I'm ready to leave when you are so I can uncover whatever two-bit charade you've got going here. Feel free to come along for the ride when I expose the medieval trappings as a fraud and you can bet I'm going to have words with that night watchman."

Fraud? Charade? She had no notion what he suggested, but his tone implied a lack of trust on his part. Understandable.

Still, she would be beyond foolish to trust a man who had appeared out of nowhere to observe her secretly in her own chamber. And to follow such a man out of her home into lands unknown with no protector, no house, no lands to provide safe haven…

Sheer madness.

"You have a mount ready?" She wasn't honestly considering it. Yet hadn't she prayed for deliverance from Burke Kendrick every night since he'd arrived at Welborne Keep with enough gold to take whatever he wished?

Who was she to dictate the way her prayers were answered? Perhaps God sent messengers in the form of devilishly handsome men whose touch made her tongue-tied.

"A mount." He lifted a skeptical eyebrow and peered down at her. "You mean a horse?"

She wouldn't let his lack of an animal deter her. Because the more she thought about this, the more she had to leave. Right now.

"I can find you a mount. It's just that when you asked me to join you for a ride I assumed you had brought your own animal with you." She moved around her chamber swiftly, packing a few things to bring with her, grabbing what few possessions she had with any sentimental value.

"It's an expression. 'Come along for the ride.'" He stared at her as if she had no sense.

But to be fair, she probably didn't. She was attempting to leave her birthplace with the man who had beheld her half-naked, but she trusted him because…he smelled favorably and his fingers were clean?

How witless and idle-headed could a woman be? She wanted to trust this man because he made her heart flutter pleasantly within her breast.

"Fine." She rolled up her belongings in a small bundle and then hesitated as she reached for her dagger on the trunk. "I'd rather like to bring a weapon. Will you be so kind as not to take this from me again?"

"Sure." He seemed to give approval, but his focus lingered on something beside her bed. The wine decanter? Her silver cup? "What's this?"

Oh. No.

Her mortification knew no bounds as he held up one of Kendrick's parting gifts.

"I…" She simply wouldn't answer. Surely he knew the purpose of the hateful object since the shape of the device practically shrieked its intent. Then again, perhaps not all men used such implements in their attentions toward women. "Pray, do not embarrass me."

Linnet had thrown it into the farthermost reaches of her trunks in the past, but evil Edana continuously resurrected the device in order to upset her. Linnet's cheeks heated unbearably as she remembered the times Kendrick had threatened her with the small tool made of horn and wood decorated with elaborate carvings.

"Holy hell." He smacked the item back onto the table. "Is that what I think it is?"

"Are you helping me depart, or not? Because I'd be much more comfortable discussing your plan than some cruel gift bestowed upon me by the man I most wish to escape."

In fact, seeing the item Kendrick had laughingly referred to as the Initiator only affirmed Linnet's desire to run as far and fast as she could. Perhaps the stranger would take her to London where she could seek shelter as a lady's maid. A very lowly lady so that her identity would not be important.

"Cruel?" He peered down at the object again, frowning. "Lady, where I come from, women collect sex toys like trading cards."

"Toys?" Heat rushed to her cheeks.

"Definitely. And I don't mean to belabor the issue, but the carvings are of interest to me because they might be a link to a criminal."

"Local law enforcement." She remembered the peculiar way he had described himself earlier and shivered at the vision of his hands upon the item she'd come to abhor. Would she still detest the object if Graham had been the one to touch her with it? "By all means, take the wicked thing far from my sight. I certainly have no desire to see it ever again."

She only wished she could rid herself of the other, even more hateful item Kendrick had bestowed upon her, but tonight, she would settle for escape.

"Fair enough." He swept up another one of her bed linens and packed the carving inside the bundle along with the wine and some fruit from her table. Rolling the supplies into a neat parcel much as she had done, he headed for the door. "Are you ready? We're going to blow this clambake so I can get back to the precinct and research those carvings."

"Linnet?" Edana Kendrick's voice floated through the door before Graham could open it. "Whom are you talking to at this hour?"

Linnet panicked, attempting to shove Graham toward the wardrobe, but he was cursedly hard to move. Before she could form a reply, Edana continued.

"I have brought reinforcements with me, my lady, since you seemed to have so much trouble opening your door to a woman who will soon be your own kin."

Already a key turned in the lock, and Graham was nowhere near the wardrobe.

Linnet's great plan for escape would be foiled before it even began. All three of her stepbrothers filled the doorway. And, upon seeing Graham Lawson LAPD, they let out a war cry that could have been heard to London and back. Saints preserve them, Graham would be killed for his transgression against her before she ever had the chance to fully savor his touch—before she ever discovered if he was the same stranger who filled her most private fantasies.

3

NORMALLY, GRAHAM WOULDN'T CARE that he'd let the bad guys one-up him in front of Linnet, since he had a bigger, better plan in mind. But the disappointment in Linnet's eyes…

Damn. How could her reaction tweak his conscience so soundly when they'd only just met?

Graham stared up at Welborne Keep from his position in the courtyard where he'd allowed himself to be taken prisoner. Linnet had even gone so far as to toss him an extra sword to defend himself when the hulking knights had gotten hold of him, since Graham had discreetly deposited his personal weapon behind her bed. And Graham hated disappointing her, but only Hollywood heroes took dumb-ass risks with civilian lives to go ballistic on their enemies. He'd underestimated Linnet's warning about her stepbrothers, still hanging tough to his personal theory that she was part of some crazy living-history exhibit at the museum.

He couldn't afford to underestimate his situation again. Not with the knowledge that the Guardians were committing more and more blatant crimes in L.A. while he hung around Welborne Keep with shackles weighing him down. He needed to choose his time and place for escape once he got a better handle on his surroundings, since he was still blown away by whatever had happened to him to drop him in a convincing-as-hell medieval setting.

There were no lights in the distance in this remote location. No planes roaring overhead. No car engines from a nearby highway. No radio broadcast drifting on the wind from far away. Not even big-money producers could make those conditions happen in L.A.

He tested the iron chains around his wrists and found them just as competent as the last time he'd checked. Five seconds ago. The scent of horses, strong whiskey and piss assailed his nose in this corner of the courtyard. A wooden arch nearby still held a dangling carcass of some poor soul who hadn't escaped the Welbornes.

From his position outside the ring of light from the bonfire, Graham watched Linnet's oafish stepbrothers argue over everything from what to do with their prisoner to which one of them could hawk a spit wad farther. Graham figured he'd have plenty of time for strategizing how to smuggle Linnet from the gargantuan castle. He didn't understand the fears that made her want to run, but they had to be substantial to prompt her to take such a risk with him.

One brother clubbed the other in the head when the argument over the spitting range got out of hand, and Graham began to think he'd made a wise move in delaying his departure from Welborne. At this rate, his

captors would all pick one another off and spare
Graham the dirty work.

Until then, he studied the padlock holding one chain
around his wrists and the other securing a cuff around
his ankle. In the deep darkness, he couldn't see much
other than a brief impression that the lock looked
absurdly simple.

Unfastening his belt, he already had a tool in mind
to pick the restraint, and promptly went to work with
the pin that normally held the belt in place. Whether or
not he wanted to believe he'd fallen through some
weirdo time door into another era, the chains holding
him to this post in the middle of the courtyard were real
enough.

Later, he'd figure out how to get back to L.A. and
share his findings about the Guardians with his department. The markings on the carving Linnet possessed
were the same symbols he'd seen on the haft of the
weapon Miguel had shown him, so there must have
been a connection at work here. The fact that Graham
had discovered the intricate signs on a twelfth-century
dildo surely explained something about his case, but he
didn't know what. Until he learned where Linnet had
gotten the sex toy and why she considered the item a
"cruel gift," Graham wouldn't be leaving the woman's
side.

And wouldn't that be an interesting conversation?

*Not only could I not stop myself from leering at you
while you undressed, I'll also need a list of your former
sex partners and the complete history of this dildo.*

Was *dildo* even a word in the twelfth century? Personal pleasure aid, maybe.

Shit.

While Linnet's stepbrothers shared a few drinks with some other guards near the gatehouse, Graham successfully picked the first lock. The chains on his wrists loosened, but he didn't slide them off yet in case one of the half-drunk bozos came over to check on him. Setting to work on the second lock, he devised a plan for getting back into the keep.

Back into Linnet's bedroom.

Because no matter that he hadn't worked in the field for a while, Graham bet he knew his way around a sword as well as her brothers. He could get Linnet out of here now that he'd taken measure of the situation and knew what they were up against.

The fact that he'd have to spend a little more time in close quarters with a sexy medieval maiden didn't exactly seem like an imposition.

LINNET FOUGHT SLEEP almost as hard as she fought the stupid tears sure to leak out of her eyes if she gave in to exhaustion and simply relaxed. She lay in bed well past midnight thinking about her strange encounter with Graham, a man who'd been prepared to steal her away from Welborne and her dreaded nuptials forever. Except that—despite his size and obvious strength—he lacked the sword prowess of a battle-hardened warrior.

He must. Else why would he allow himself to be taken so easily? Saints protect the poor man. There was no telling what end he would come to in the hands of Hugo, Douglas and John. Her father's first wife had been a great beauty by all accounts, but she had spawned sons of unusually dim wit. Yet her father had loved them far more than the girl-child offered by his second wife. A girl as weak as her mother, in his eyes. William of Welborne had never counted intelligence as a strength.

More's the pity.

But after seeing Graham give in to her brothers without a fight, perhaps her father had understood a key to success that she had missed. All the intelligence in the world could not buy a man the lands and respect that a strong sword arm could.

Closing her eyes at last, she swiped away a lone tear she could not help. Graham would suffer bitterly for his presence in her bedchamber, but she could not rely on a quick end for him. He would probably be tortured until he revealed his true purpose and his method of entering the keep once her brothers were sober enough to enjoy their blood sport. She didn't even have the heart to employ her skill with the Sight to discover if that fate might be true.

Linnet only hoped Graham could convince her brothers more effectively than he'd convinced her that he could not remember how he'd come to be in her wardrobe. Unable to think about Graham's clean hands or startlingly pale blue eyes anymore if she did not wish to weep, Linnet focused on pushing air in and out of her lungs slowly. Rhythmically. Only sleep would take her away from the lingering regrets about what might have been if she'd been able to escape her future as Lady Kendrick.

But fitful dreams followed, keeping her tossing and turning until she could almost imagine she smelled the clean scent of Graham's skin. The notion calmed her, soothed her and excited her at the same time.

"Linnet." The dream voice—Graham's voice—prodded her to awaken. To open her eyes and remain quiet.

But she knew if she awoke, he would be gone and she would be left imagining his demise at her brothers' hands. No, better to enjoy these moments with him where he was safe and warm and sliding into her sheets beside her, urging compliance.

Did the man know how readily she would comply in other ways?

Ah, those thoughts were wicked and yet she relished them. Sex should not be a dreaded chore or a brutal coupling as she suspected—nay, knew—a union with Kendrick would be. Sex should thrill and excite, a welcome opportunity to physically indulge oneself completely....

Graham's hands brushed along her arm and up her shoulder the way it had in other half-remembered dreams. She could imagine the feel of those hands perfectly, since he had touched her thus earlier. Only now, without the barrier of her surcoat, she could savor the warm strength of his callused palms skimming along one bare arm. He paused at the narrow shoulder strap of her nightrail, testing the delicate fabric as if he enjoyed the feel of it. Enjoyed the feel of her *through the material.*

If only he were real. She would wrestle him into her bed and...

"Linnet." *The voice loomed nearer and more urgent.*

And truly, she began to feel quite urgent about the matter as well. Heat stirred inside her belly, spreading over her thighs and her breasts. She could not get close enough to him.

Ready for more of his touch, she guided his hand down the front of her, off her shoulder and to the curve of her breast. He paused for a moment, as if unsure that he should take such a liberty, but then, he cupped the mound through the fine linen and scraped his thumb boldly across the nipple.

The pleasure twisted sharply inside her, her reaction swift and hungry. She arched back wantonly, shamelessly edging her rump closer to his groin when the pinch of metal along her hip reminded her of all she could not have.

Even in her dream, curse it all. Frustrated tears burned her eyes.

"Holy hell." *Graham's voice was no longer soft and gentle, although he still whispered. A harsh note rasped through his words as he dipped a hand lower to explore the metal confinement her betrothed had insisted she wear while he was at war.*

Unnerved, Linnet shook herself...

...and faced Graham Lawson. Very much alive and in her bed.

"Devil take you!" She scrambled back from him, out of his grasp and off the feather-tick mattress, dragging a blanket with her to cover herself. "How long have you been there?"

Her heart beat furiously, her head spinning as she attempted to separate reality from her dream. She'd wanted more of his touch, yet his knowledge of her secret—her chastity belt—embarrassed her.

"How can you sleep in metal?" He rose to his knees, his striped shirt now smudged with dirt and torn at the neck. His whole demeanor struck her as darker and more dangerous, but perhaps that arose from her knowledge that he had somehow escaped her battle-hardened brothers and lived to tell the tale.

Perhaps there was more warrior prowess to this man than she'd initially perceived.

"I can see that *you* didn't wish to sleep in metal. How in Hades did you get out of the irons?" If he could free himself from a padlock, what might he be able to do for her dilemma?

The thought made her shiver in pleasant anticipation and she feared not the least of the sensation was a vision of herself exposing her bare body to this man so that he might…help her.

"I told you I would get you out of here." Even in the pale light of the moon, she could see his smile. His teeth stood out whitely against his skin. "My discussion with your brothers was only a minor delay. Do you still have your belongings packed?"

Dear God, he was serious. Excitement of a new and different kind flowed through her veins, easing the dark heat that his touch had excited.

"I am very much prepared." She'd kept their bundles stowed beneath her bed only because she couldn't bear to admit their plan wasn't meant to be. "But Hugo took the sword I tossed you. Do you have another?"

She didn't even want to consider the possibility that he did not know how to wield one.

"I'll take what I need from one of the guys sleeping in your hall. There's got to be fifty men sacked out there—most of them armed." He stared at her for a long moment. "But we can't leave until you're dressed. Come on."

He made an impatient gesture that somehow implied a need for speed.

"Then turn around." She clutched her blanket securely to her chest, dismayed to feel her pulse galloping like a steed in the wild. "I cannot dress until you provide me a bit of privacy. And this time, you may not steal secret looks."

If she ever disrobed in front of this man again, she would rather be able to enjoy every delicious moment of it. Rogue memories of his touch on her breast fanned the heat within.

Sliding off the bed, he pivoted on his heel, presenting her with his back.

"Really? You might want to reconsider your thinking on that, lady, since it was thoughts of you naked that inspired me to bust free of the chains and get back in your bedroom."

She yanked a fresh kirtle from her trunk and tugged it over her head, leaving her nightrail in place for now since she would not risk Graham turning around.

"You, sir, are highly inappropriate." She elbowed her way into a surcoat and realized belatedly she wouldn't be able to tie the laces without help. And since Edana had elected to sleep elsewhere given Linnet's anger with her, the only source of assistance would be…

She peered over her shoulder, only to discover Graham watching her.

"Hey, I only turned a second ago when I heard the rustling stop. I assumed you must be dressed." He stepped closer, his dark, intimate gaze seeming to imagine her *without* her garments. "Want help?"

Yes. But even more so, she wanted to feel his hands again. Surely she only experienced this level of heat with a stranger because her unfortunate sexual restraints made her all the more—eager.

"It seems I don't have a choice." She lifted her arm enough to allow him access to the laces up one side of the garment. "You didn't kill my stepbrothers, did you?" She regretted that she had not thought to ask sooner, but her brain had been muddled ever since waking. At his emphatic denial, she continued, "And how did you know Edana wouldn't be in my chamber just now?"

"Why would she be in here?" He shrugged, his eyebrows furrowing in concentration.

The warmth of his hands near such a vulnerable spot made her shiver.

"She is my maid. Where else would she sleep?" Linnet turned as he finished one side so that he could work on the other. "You are obviously a stranger to England. May I ask where you call home?"

"You wouldn't believe me if I told you." He yanked a bit too hard on one of the laces, causing her to stumble slightly. "Sorry. These outfits of yours… Damn."

"They are not as simple as men's clothes, I fear."

"Mostly they're just sexy as hell." He finished securing the ties and lowered his hands. "Aren't you scared of riding off into the sunset with me?"

"If we wait until sunset, yes. Are you mad? We need to leave now, under cover of darkness, before my kinsmen discover you are no longer their prisoner."

Realizing she would have to double her efforts to ensure they got away safely, Linnet retrieved her ink and parchment to sketch a rough map of the grounds. Graham might be an attractive man who fired her insides with his touch, but he was no strategist.

Since failure was not an option, she would simply apply whatever tactical knowledge she could to his plan.

And although she could swear he swallowed back a laugh at her attempts to help him, she noticed he listened carefully as she outlined her ideas.

IF LINNET WELBORNE LIVED in L.A. in the twenty-first century, she could have been a kick-ass detective. Or possibly a very clever criminal, given her notes on by-passing the guards along the keep's walls.

Graham knew she thought he was a piss-poor excuse for a knight since he hadn't fought off her stepbrothers earlier, but he'd never minded being underestimated. Better to pleasantly surprise someone with his capability at the pivotal moment than to devastate them with a failure they hadn't seen coming. Maybe this way Linnet would be all the more prepared for whatever hardships they faced if she thought she'd have to help him.

But he still had a blade strapped to his ankle that the Welborne wastrels had never thought to look for and he'd easily picked off an extra sword and a dagger from the sleeping dudes in the great hall as they'd left the castle. Between those weapons and his own sword that Linnet had saved for him, he figured he'd give anyone who came upon them a run for their money.

Now, as they climbed down the lowest section of the keep's walls using a ladder hidden on the parapets from a long-ago siege, Graham couldn't take his eyes off Linnet's form descending above him. They'd worked in silence ever since they'd left her room, relying on their predetermined plan to get them this far. Their biggest obstacle would be finding horses to put as much distance as possible between them and the keep, but Linnet swore she knew where they could find shelter.

Catching her in his arms as she reached the bottom rung, Graham felt her swift intake of breath, but she did not cry out. She was made of steely stuff, this woman.

And speaking of steely, he couldn't wait to ask her what was up with the metal belt she wore beneath her clothes. He'd double-checked her pack before they'd left and found the carving still inside—his key to linking the modern Guardians to ancient rituals, maybe.

Pulling Linnet along with him, they ran full out through the damp meadow grasses surrounding the walls, the scent of the sea heavy in the cool night air.

When they finally reached the shelter of the woods, they could at least speak, even if they had to move quickly.

"If you knew that ladder was there all this time, why didn't you ever try to escape on your own?" Graham couldn't understand so many things about her, but he found himself wanting to figure her out, to demystify the hints of prickly toughness that went hand in hand with reticence that made her intriguing.

"It would have been a much bigger risk without you. A woman traveling alone, without a protector is— Can a woman travel alone in your lands?" She paused for a moment in their fast walk through the trees where they traveled east toward this shelter she assured him awaited them.

Apparently she thought him from some far-off and exotic country, which suited him fine.

"Yeah. Actually, they can." Except for when street scum like the Guardians crawled out of the sewers to terrorize a city with multiple abductions. "But it always pays to be cautious. You were smart to wait for an extra set of hands."

Her soft gulp of laughter surprised him.

"On the contrary, I have found your hands create a great deal of trouble for me." She ducked under a low branch with him, her gaze fastened on the path in front of them.

She wasn't flirting with him, was she? He wrote off the thought as wishful thinking since she'd seemed pretty panicked at the idea of finding him in her bed earlier.

"Yet you weren't afraid to leave your home, your stepbrothers' protection?" He would never hurt her, but she had no way of knowing that for certain. She took a huge risk to walk out into the darkened forest with a total stranger.

Slowing her pace, she turned to face him, her long hair unbound and wild around her shoulders with bits of leaves decorating the strands.

"I am very afraid to leave my home. But I have arrived at a point in my life where it would be far more dangerous to stay."

4

"WHAT DANGERS COULD POSSIBLY chase you from home when you have three Neanderthal siblings to scare away anyone who comes near?"

Linnet's heart still pounded from their escape, their decision to leave on foot putting them more at risk of capture if they didn't make haste. Even so, the need to unburden herself urged her to speak. Share with someone the hell her life had become these last three years.

"Neanderthal." She pronounced the foreign word carefully as she ducked under a low-hanging branch, wishing she understood this curious stranger. "You mean big?"

"Neanderthal man lived in the Middle Paleolithic period." He stared at her hard, his gaze unrelenting in the scant moonlight filtering through the leafy canopy of hazel, oak and ash trees. "Which could be where I'll end up if I'm not more cautious around old paintings."

Thoroughly confused, she couldn't even begin to decipher his meaning, so she pointed the direction to her younger brother's fortified holding where he maintained a small store of weapons and supplies. The journey would be more perilous in the dark, but at least the temperatures remained mild and pleasant as the year approached Midsummer.

Once they made it to the holding, they would be safe for a few days. They could arm themselves more heavily until she could plan a future for herself without any support from kin. She prayed her head would clear enough to think once she was out from under a constant shadow of fear.

"The dwelling I mentioned is this way, about ten leagues. We could be there in a trice if we had taken the horses." One day, her young brother would build on the lands with his share of the profits from her marriage to Kendrick, but until then, he'd vowed to keep her safe along with her other brothers until her betrothed returned. Her lifelong servitude would buy her brothers' wealth. Prestige.

"There was no simple way to ride out the main gate. We would have had to incapacitate several watch guards and even so it would have been a risk." Graham picked out a path in the dark, his keen eyes finding the worn trail the deer took to a nearby pond. "Can you walk in those shoes?"

"Of course." She felt every root and downfallen branch in the thin slippers, but she welcomed the physical discomfort after months of increasing mental anguish in a life full of inconsequential luxuries. "Now that I am free, there is a fair chance I can fly if necessary."

The clean air was scented with pine and not the stench of her brothers and their animals. She inhaled deep breaths, but in addition to pine, she caught *his* scent as he waited for her in the darkness. Awareness skittered through her as she realized she was completely alone with this man—a circumstance forbidden to unwed women in general and her in particular.

"Do they abuse you?" Graham held a branch aside for her as they picked their way through the darkened woods.

"My craven kin? They do not dare to lay a finger on me." No one save wicked Edana had touched her in years. Which perhaps accounted for the reason her blood quickened at Graham's nearness. "My reasons for wanting to leave have naught to do with my kin, repugnant though they might be."

She stayed close to him as they moved through the dense forest. The brush around their feet rustled with animals seeking shelter. Now and then she spied small eyes upon them from the trees.

"Then what? You're sick of not having indoor plumbing or central heat in a windy old castle?"

Once again she couldn't quite fathom his words, but she suspected he grew impatient from his brusque tone.

"I am leaving to escape a doomed marriage and a betrothed whom I loathe." Telling him was a risk. She could not afford to have him bring her back to Welborne for the sake of a reward, but she suspected a man like Graham would not be easily swayed to follow any path save his own. Not many men would listen to a woman's wishes, let alone honor them, and yet he had. Perhaps she misjudged him, but in her mind that decision seemed to hint at a nobility of character.

Graham halted his tromp through the forest so suddenly she all but ran into his broad back. He pivoted slowly, his movements unsettlingly silent.

"You're *married?*"

"Nay." His intense scrutiny made her uneasy. Or perhaps it was his nearness that merely made her skin tingle. "But I am promised to a man whose touch I fear."

"Fear his touch?" He shook his head in disbelief. "Is this some kind of pseudo-virginal protest of a big, bad man? Because if you're playing me to make some dumb guy jealous—"

"I do not play." She might not understand all his words, but she certainly knew what he implied. That she indulged girlish ploys of favor. "I am not playing."

"Then why are you up to your eyeballs in sex toys and lounging in bed wearing a chastity belt? You seem like you're playing plenty of adult games to me, and the last thing I need is to get mixed up in a couple's personal business so I can get skewered by a pissed-off boy-friend."

Embarrassment fled as anger roared to life.

"You call this curse that I bear a game?" Her raised voice might echo straight back to Welborne for all she knew, but she could not temper the swell of fears and fury long suppressed. "I would like to see you don such an inhumane contraption for years on end. I would like to see you offer your untouched, youthful body to a lecherous old man to drool over while he locks you into painful captivity with no regard that your hips might grow more round or that you might never sit a horse without pain or run unfettered and free through spring grasses, or—"

He reached for her in the darkness, his hand grazing her shoulder in simple kindness. "I'm sorry."

The words hardly seemed enough to stem the tide of resentment, but they were more than she'd ever been offered in the past. And combined with his touch…the gesture touched her heart as much as her person.

"I only meant to assure you that I do not play." She had not meant to unleash so much unhappiness upon him. Her suffering was her own. But she wanted to be very clear on this one point. "My need to leave is no jest."

"This guy you're supposed to marry locked you into that metal belt?" He did not sound disbelieving so much as a man intent on setting his facts straight. "And he did this *years* ago?"

Peering over her shoulder, she saw no sign of movement from the direction they'd come, but she did not wish to take any chances if perhaps her voice had carried.

"A bit more than three years. May we discuss this while we walk?" She'd rather not discuss it at all, but Graham was a persistent sort and she found herself committed to an unusual relationship with the stranger. She owed him some explanation for her escape.

Nodding, he turned back to the path and proceeded through the trees.

"But if you expect me to be the mastermind behind your vanishing act, I think you ought to fill me in on this would-be husband of yours so I know what I'm up against. Where the hell is this guy and how soon will he come looking for you?"

"He's been away on Crusade ever since he left me locked in a vile ring of steel, but my stepbrothers have informed me that Kendrick returns with some of his best knights and he should reach Welborne in a few days' time."

"Kendrick?"

Curses bubbled to her lips at her misstep, but she did not speak them. She had never been good at keeping secrets, so it did not surprise her that she'd fumbled her future overlord's identity already. She only hoped Graham would not use the knowledge to betray her.

"Burke Kendrick, son of a powerful lord with lands from Wales to London. Burke seeks to distinguish himself in service to the Lion-Heart, perhaps so that the king does not frown upon the Kendrick penchant for greedily besieging peaceful keeps on neighboring lands in a ceaseless effort to build their wealth and fame." Linnet thought Kendrick would enjoy nothing more than the power to do whatever he wished, whenever he wished, a power normally reserved for kings.

"And you think he returns to set up house with you?"

"I think he comes to claim me in every way possible." She could not abide the thought after seeing hints of her betrothed's brutal nature. "And while that means I might at last see the end of the cursed metal about my waist, I find I'd far rather live a life in delicate iron than to submit to a man who speaks with his fists rather than his tongue."

"Meaning what, exactly? He beat the crap out of your brothers to win your hand?" He peered over his shoulder but did not pause their race through the forest. "Or has he beaten you?"

"The man could not have gotten me naked without the use of beastly force." She'd been mortified. Enraged. And her worthless kin had done nothing to protect her from Kendrick's presumption.

Ahead of her in the darkness, Graham cursed in that strange accent she'd already come to recognize, the words all the more profane-sounding for the guttural way he articulated the language. His tone left no mistake what a "sorry piece of shit" might be, and Linnet found herself comforted at the outpouring of anger on her behalf.

"So he beat you and locked you up in a chastity-enforcing torture device. Weren't you a little concerned about what this prince among men would have to say about you keeping sensual aids at your bedside like that carved bit of horn I took from your bedroom earlier?"

"Sensual aids?" She knew that he must refer to the wicked device Kendrick had left behind, but she wondered at Graham's words.

He took her hand to assist her over a fallen tree limb as they reached a thin stream of water cutting through the forest.

"Your cheeks colored five shades of red when I asked about the carved piece earlier, so let's skip the shy medieval-maiden routine where the dildo is concerned, okay? I'm guessing you can't use it if you've been locked up like a sexual martyr for three years, but I'm guessing you know exactly what it's used for."

"Your speech is foreign to me, sir, and yet I gather you are hoping to cause me discomfort with your forthright words." She held his hand for no longer than necessary, leery of depending on him for anything and determined not to let him cause her unease with his strange conversational topics. "Is it common in your land to purposefully distress a woman in the course of conversation?"

"I'm not trying to cause you distress." He turned sharply to the west at a small clearing and then backtracked toward the east to break a few branches in the wrong direction before he rejoined her. "I'm trying to figure out if the carvings on that piece of horn are related to a case I'm working on."

A case? She didn't bother to ask. By now her slippers were soaked and a sharp stick had punctured a hole through the velvet into her foot. They'd hastened their steps until they nearly ran through the darkness, but even so, they had covered little ground.

"I know nothing of the carvings," she told him honestly, wishing they could have risked an escape on horseback for the sake of speed as much as her feet. "In truth, I refuse to look at the device since my despised betrothed presented it to me as a parting gift."

"The man who snaps you in a chastity belt gives you *that* as a gift? What kind of sadistic bastard—"

He stopped short, as he turned on her once again.

"I want you to think carefully about this, Linnet." He

flipped the traveling sack with her scant possessions onto his other shoulder as he faced her. "Do you have any reason to believe this fiancé of yours is involved in some sort of sex cult?"

GRAHAM ADMITTED his interrogation skills had never been all that keen since he was a man who favored action over words. But he'd really struck out big-time asking his unlikely traveling companion about a sex cult.

They tromped through an endless meadow just past daybreak, their last miles of travel a silent trip after Linnet had frozen at his abrupt question. For all he knew, she could have been sexually traumatized by this freak of nature her stepbrothers had consigned her to for a husband. Scratch that. Being locked into a chastity belt for three years probably counted as sexual trauma by itself, so Graham had been an idiot to hound her on the sex angle.

Still, a connection between the Guardians and this Burke Kendrick guy remained. Why else would Graham have fallen ass-backward into this weird time fugue? There had to be some cosmic balance at work behind his banishment to a world with no airplanes, cell-phone towers or paved roads. Those bits of evidence convinced him something strange had happened to him more strongly than waking up in Linnet's closet or discovering that his cell-phone screen remained utterly blank even though it was charged.

"There is the holding." Linnet paused beside him, pointing toward another thicket of trees ahead. "Can you see the roof?"

The outline of the dwelling was evident now that his eye sought it, but the structure hid well in the landscape. He had to admit he looked forward to sitting still for a few hours—hell, a few days—to sort out his head and think through what to do with Linnet. He needed to scout out the terrain and get a handle on a safe place to take her if this pervert fiancé of hers was as bad as she thought.

"I can't believe I'm in freaking England." Seeing the fortified structure on the horizon drove home the point he'd been denying all night. The morning light made it impossible to think he could be anywhere in the whole state of California, or anywhere in the world in the twenty-first century.

He'd walked right into a history textbook and he didn't have the first clue how to get back out. Not that he wanted to—yet. First he'd find the clues he'd come to the Getty Center seeking, and then he'd make sure Linnet was safe. Once that was accomplished, he'd tackle the matter of returning to life as he knew it.

"I can't believe I might elude Kendrick." She turned to grin at him and her smile almost knocked him on his butt.

Linnet of Welborne didn't need two hours in a Hollywood makeup chair. She had the medieval "it" factor coming out her ears.

And the sex appeal? Off the charts. Even when she'd been tromping through the woods all night. If he hadn't been semisensitive to whatever trauma this Kendrick guy had put her through, Graham might have been tempted to wonder how sex-starved and aggressive a woman would be after three years of enforced chastity. Knowing he couldn't have her only made him want her more and shamed him at the same time since no woman deserved that damned contraption she bore.

"You've already eluded him." He would not dwell on thoughts of fulfilling Linnet's every suppressed fantasy since he had an investigation to close and eight hundred years to traverse in order to do the job.

"For now." Her smile disappeared and she trudged forward.

Limping?

"Did you hurt your foot?" He couldn't see her legs with her heavy, mud-splattered skirts dragging along the grasses, but her stride was uneven, one shoulder dipping lower than the other as she walked.

"I fear my shoes were not worthy of the trip." She limped onward toward the towering stone house.

Graham couldn't help but remember his ex-girlfriend the movie extra would call in sick if her face broke out. And while he didn't blame her, considering the fiercely competitive atmosphere of Hollywood, he also thought it ironic that the proverbial damsel in distress had scaled her own castle walls to escape and walked for miles in the dark on injured feet. The fainting and worshipful historical stereotype for women was obviously a myth.

That didn't mean he couldn't play white knight once in a while. Did it?

"Let me give you a hand." He caught up to her in quick strides and scooped her off her feet.

She made a muffled yelp of surprise but didn't protest.

"You could have given me a warning." She held herself upright and rigid against him.

"You could have given *me* a damn warning you were hurt. I could have given you a lift a long time ago." He quickened his step, thinking he shouldn't get involved with a woman whose historical context defied all possible dating scenarios. Bad enough to live on opposite coasts from the object of your affection, but nine centuries apart?

Not bloody likely.

Still, as his fingers gripped soft curves, he wondered if a medieval woman could be persuaded to indulge in a one-time fling.

"I have not been outside the walls of Welborne since my betrothal." She gestured toward the entrance of the dwelling as they approached. "The pain in my feet is soothed by the knowledge I am free for a little while."

"Why not forever? I can help you find a place to stay if you think your family will look for you here." Or so he hoped, since he still hadn't figured out what had happened to him and where he was. Most of the time, he was totally buying into the wormhole-in-time theory. But he refused to waste time scratching his head about the matter when he was definitely discovering some clues to the Guardians.

Besides, he was in no hurry to leave this woman, be she real or fantasy.

"They will search here in a few days at the most. I have dreamed for six nights straight that my betrothed rides for England, and my brothers are convinced he's already reached our shores." She wriggled in an obvious desire to stand on her own feet as they reached the threshold to the house. "That is why I'd prefer we leave no signs of our presence, if that is possible."

He halted her hand when she would have reached for the doorknob.

"It's very possible. But the last thing we'd want to do is enter through the front door. Is there another way in?"

"There is an entrance on the other side, but it is surrounded by thorny hedges to prevent intruders. This entrance used to be protected in that way, too, but my youngest brother grew impatient in trimming the bushes and he ripped them all out at the roots."

He backed away from the house to size it up and then searched the outbuildings for some sort of tool to break in discreetly so they could rest and regroup. His job as a cop had prepared him well for a life of crime, although breaking and entering in this case were totally justified.

Lodging a plank of wood at an angle to a low wall above the first level, Graham climbed onto the house and scouted means of entry from above. He found one easily, a low door from the makeshift battlement that was more like a second-story porch along the outer wall.

"Follow me," he called down to Linnet even as he walked back to give her a hand. "We leave no dust disturbed on the lower level this way. Your stepbrothers might not think to check the second story if the first looks untouched."

He teetered his way down the plank to help her walk the narrow path, not trusting her to make the trek with an injured foot.

"Very clever," she admitted, admiration shining in her eyes for a moment before she looked down at the potentially treacherous walkway.

And damn but the admiration felt nice.

"I've got you." He looped his arm around her waist to walk her sideways along the plank, his role as white knight growing on him. No wonder Brendan Jameson dug the hero roles.

Playing savior kicked ass.

Graham might be tempted to hang out in the twelfth century and explore his inner knight with Linnet as incentive. Except that he'd ended up here to play hero to those abducted women in L.A. who needed his investigative skills more than Linnet needed a conspirator in her escape. And as his hands molded around her generous curves that had never been restrained by underwires or spandex, he had to admit that for the first time in ten years, he seriously regretted his line of work.

5

LINNET DREW SHALLOW BREATHS in those heated moments in Graham's arms. His hands burned through her clothes to singe her skin, but somehow the shallow inhalation prevented his fingers from sinking deeper into her softness.

She couldn't shake the sense that if she allowed his hands to venture farther, she would never be free of a desire for more. When she'd been certain her brothers would kill him, she'd craved his touch one last time. But now that his hands held her to him with such dizzying effect, she began to fear the tide of emotions sure to follow if she indulged this desire.

Bad enough she was prepared to risk her own neck to Kendrick's wrath. She could not jeopardize Graham's after all he'd done to help her.

"Careful," he warned, slowing his pace as they reached the juncture of the plank board and the protruding battlement on the second level.

She didn't dare to look down, keeping her eyes focused on Graham as he reached for her, pulled her in from the ledge and onto stable ground.

Too bad her heart did not steady as well.

The smart thing to do would have been to retreat from his grip. To step out of his arms and away from the temptation he presented. But his hands encircled her waist the same way they had when he'd helped her leap from the low wall onto the second-floor parapet covered in limestone gravel.

"Let me break you out of this." Graham's voice was low and urgent and not at all romantic.

Too late, she realized his hands spanned her hips to rest lightly on the chastity belt. Her embarrassment was lessened by an answering surge of eagerness. And more than a little desire.

"You really think you could set me free?" Even as she asked, she knew he could, but she hadn't dared to hope for so long. This man from a strange land possessed strengths she had only just begun to discover. "The lock is more sophisticated than the one on the irons my brothers possess."

Graham released her to peer briefly over the parapet and then drag the plank they'd climbed onto the second story where he hid it behind the low wall.

"How do you know it's more sophisticated?"

"Just a guess. Kendrick possesses the best of everything and the belt came from him." She shrugged, savoring the freedom of the fresh morning breeze and the new surroundings that seemed full of possibilities. "Besides, I tried the keys to my brothers' shackles, and it did not work on this torturous device that I wear."

"I have something to show you that might convince

you I can bust you loose. Should we go inside to make sure no one will see us?"

In spite of all the hours outdoors and the ache in her feet, she did not wish to leave the fresh scents and sunshine dawning on the first day of her future.

"I would prefer to remain here. There is no road nearby for travelers to see us and I find myself loath to leave the sense of freedom of the day." If her family found them tomorrow, or if Kendrick arrived to retrieve her, she wanted to hoard as many happy memories as she could from her brief taste of liberty.

"The wall would hide us from sight if we took a seat." Graham seemed sure of himself here, his assessing eye missing nothing as he weighed the situation. "Why don't we open the door to the house and sit on the threshold so if we need to retreat quickly we can?"

Arguing seemed selfish and—quite possibly— futile, so she followed him to the tall doors leading into an upstairs sleeping chamber. The house smelled musty and unused, no surprise since her youngest brother did not make use of the family home after their father had died. All the Welborne manpower had been spent keeping their valuable sister under lock and key.

Linnet had only been here once before, when her mother had been dying and her father had sent her from Welborne Keep as if she were as contagious as a leper. He had not minded when Linnet had begged to attend her mother since she was apparently as expendable as the wife he'd only wed for her wealth.

"Thank you," she blurted as she sat beside him on

the wooden threshold worn smooth by many men's boots. Her own slippers had paced here countless hours as she prayed for her mother's recovery. "I appreciate you bringing me here. I know you take a great risk to do so."

"The risks are negligible for me. My line of work is all about taking calculated chances." He reached into a flap of material on the back of his hip and withdrew a shiny metal object—a slender box with rounded ends. "I used my belt to pick the lock on my shackles last night, but only because I couldn't reach my pocketknife."

He flipped open a shiny blade from one end of the thin tool.

"A dagger that folds into itself." The weapon was not thick enough to take into battle, but it was all the more useful for its sleek casing. "A cursedly clever device."

"But wait. There's more." He reached into the narrow box and tugged out another tool. "Act now, and you also get a screwdriver."

A tiny stick popped out beside the knife, followed in quick succession by a series of other implements of varying shapes and sizes, the likes of which she had never seen. Some looked to be for cutting, while others had a metal loop or a spiral of steel.

"You possess a treasure trove in this clever box." She marveled over the miniature size of the items. "Any chatelaine would love such a prize."

"Yeah, well, if I knew I was coming I would have stopped off at Wal-Mart for a whole case." He let her study the tool and work the smooth hinges for a long moment before he drove home his point. "Between the screwdriver and the nail file, I can have you out of that belt in ten minutes, max."

"I would like that, but I fear such a task would be better undertaken by a woman, or someone close to me."

She picked at the folds of her long skirts, the overhang from the eaves shielding her face from the sun on their threshold perch.

"Because I might glimpse two square inches of your naked hip? Don't you think you owe it to yourself to toss off the shackles and claim your life instead of worrying about what I might see?" He didn't move closer or try to intimidate her into seeing his point of view. If anything, he seemed content to let his words be the more forceful persuasion while his well-muscled arms rested easily at his sides.

She couldn't possibly consider his suggestion that she take off all her clothes for him to manipulate a lock positioned in the most private of places. Just the thought of such intimacy should make her shudder after the brutal way Kendrick had forced the foul restraint on her. But instead of repulsing her, the idea fascinated her with the raw power of sexual curiosity. Especially when she knew Graham's hands to be so capable.

Slowly becoming aware of the long silence, she rushed to fill the air with some sort of response.

"Perhaps while I am thinking it over, you would be so kind as to explain this Walmart. Is he a silversmith in your land?"

"Linnet." He took her hand in his in a touch meant to soothe, or perhaps just to hold her interest.

Little did he know, he was the cause of all her distraction. Now that they were behind the walls of the holding, her fears of her brothers had eased enough to make way for new worries. Her heart tripped twice before finding its rhythm again. She realized at that moment she wanted to kiss Graham Lawson LAPD, and she had no idea where he came from or what he was doing here.

Or when he might leave her to face an uncertain future alone.

"Perhaps if you allowed me to borrow your collection of tools, I could pick the lock for myself." She'd meant to question him more about Walmart and the land of his birth, but she could not deny a keen interest in releasing the bands of her self-contained prison.

"I know you want to do this yourself, but I'm experienced with picking locks for reasons I don't want to get into right now. I can get you out faster than you can say the alphabet backward and we'll make sure you stay covered the whole time."

"You spied on me while I was changing clothes back at Welborne Keep. Why would I ever trust you to play the chivalrous knight now?"

"That was before I realized the chastity belt was a barbaric attempt to control you instead of some weirdo sex game you played with a lover." He squeezed her fingers lightly. "Now that I know how much of a head game this has been for you for three years, I would never try to sneak a peek or cop a feel. I just want to help."

The warmth of his hands wore down her defenses, but the quiet sincerity in his eyes delivered the final blow to her resistance.

How could she say no to a man with eyes the color of an endless summer sky? She just might take flight if she stared into his gaze long enough.

"I like the idea of defeating Kendrick in this," she admitted, freeing her hands from his before she agreed to anything else. "Why don't we make a deal that if I agree to let you try unfastening the lock, you promise to tell me all about the lands of your kinsmen?"

He hesitated for the briefest of moments, causing her to wonder what secrets he kept.

"Deal. But you go first. I'm not saying anything until I spring you out of there and you're running through the daisies like a ten-year-old." He craned his neck to see behind them into the old bedchamber. "All we need is a place for you to lie down so we can get to work."

THEY GOT AS FAR AS THE RAISED platform where a pallet could be placed in the bedchamber before Linnet spun on her heel and started doling out reasons for why they should wait to go through with his plan. Eyes wide with worry, she began running through a litany of excuses for delaying her release from captivity. The belt wasn't all that uncomfortable. She didn't want him to break "his steely miracle" called a pocketknife on her behalf. But when she launched into an explanation about not wanting to involve him in a scheme sure to ignite the wrath of her betrothed, Graham could keep quiet no longer on the subject.

"Don't you dare be afraid for me." He'd tried gentle persuasion and logic, but apparently he couldn't afford to hold anything back in this debate. "If you want to be scared for yourself, go right ahead. That I can understand. But don't back out of this because of some groundless fear for me."

He stood over her as she sank to the platform where a bed should be. The fortified holding was all but barren inside, although a few rolled tapestries hid behind an oak chest at the foot of the raised stone pallet.

"The man I'm bound to is arguably the most fearsome warrior in the Lion-Heart's realm. His sword prowess is legendary and his ruthlessness well known."

"News flash, babe. My sword prowess is pretty freaking legendary where I come from, too, and I have ten years of experience keeping innocent people safe from bad guys. Creeps like Kendrick are the reason I went into law enforcement." At her confused expression, he slowed down his tirade to explain. "Where I come from, I'm like a sheriff."

"You serve your king?"

And wouldn't his precinct commander just love that comparison?

"Something like that. The point is, if I ever meet your former fiancé, it's going to be him who regrets the encounter, not me. I happen to contain a lot of pent-up anger over men who abuse women." He didn't want to think about the cases he'd seen in the past, domestic-violence calls where he couldn't do a damn thing to help women in dangerous positions because they wouldn't help themselves by pressing charges.

"I haven't been abused," she protested, perhaps not liking the mental picture of herself as a victim.

"Bad guys don't always leave bruises." He'd missed a case like that right under his own nose once. An oversight he'd never forgotten because the victim had been his mother and he'd been too dazzled by the prospect of a dad that he'd missed how withdrawn and unhappy his mother had become over the years of a miserable relationship.

He'd learned the hard way that some men were better at hiding their predatory nature than others.

"Graham?" Linnet's voice called him back from dark musings and regrets he'd never be able to right.

She stared up at him without fear now, her green eyes altered from nervous to resolved.

"I doubted you before when my brothers seemed to overtake you, but you escaped the brute strength of three men with cunning." She smiled and dazzled the hell out of him. "I will not doubt you again."

If she'd had any dragons to slay at that moment, Graham figured he probably would have faced the fire-breathing kind head-on for the chance to keep her smiling and safe.

"What about you? Are you going to keep underestimating yourself, or are you going to tell your fiancé to go to hell—not in so many words, but in your actions?"

Graham knew better than to get involved in a case,

and that's how he had to view this interlude with Linnet. In the time that he'd known her, she'd morphed from a fantasy woman to someone he needed to protect.

He pressed his advantage when she did not respond immediately.

"Besides, once I break you loose of the metal, you'll be able to haul ass away from him if he ever shows his face around you again. Think how much faster you'll be able to move without an impediment dragging you down."

"You are a most unusual man, Graham Lawson. You've not only talked me into baring half my body to your talented hands, but now you have me believing I would be a coward if I did not do so."

If he hadn't been so hard-bitten by the image of Linnet undressing for the sake of his touch, he might have refuted her words. As it was, he promptly swallowed his tongue and began to wonder just who was making whom more nervous.

This woman was young. Not jailbait young, but if she'd been in the twenty-first century, she would be just barely out of college. Sure she was wise beyond her years, considering the life she'd led, but Graham didn't want to start having more suggestive daydreams about her.

And considering the track record he had with women—his ex a fine example of the females he'd crossed paths with before—he really ought to at least consider that Linnet might be using him the same way his ex had used him to obtain her dream role and meet Brendan Jameson.

"I'm ready when you are." He found himself reaching for his pocketknife in spite of his reservations, because she needed him to be strong and sure of himself when she started peeling off her clothes and not taunted by erotic thoughts.

Together they laid out the blanket she'd packed from her bedroom back at her brother's castle. She'd brought food and wine, two clean blankets, some extra clothes that took up way too much room and the sex toy with the carvings he still needed to study. Graham had brought his sword along with a handful of other weapons he'd swiped from Welborne Keep. He didn't necessarily need more blades since he could only swing one at a time, but he figured the less weaponry he left with the enemy, the better.

"I grow more milk-livered by the moment." Linnet spun on her heel in a swirl of green and yellow skirts, her under- and over-dresses spinning around her ankles like Saturn's rings. "I do not wish you to think me craven, but the idea of removing clothes is… That is, the last time I did so with a man—"

"Did he do more than…beat you?" As if that hadn't been bad enough. Fury at the last man to touch her choked him, but he dug deep to keep his voice calm. Level. If she'd been raped, she would surely have emotional issues Graham couldn't overcome with his limited knowledge of victim psychology.

"Nay. But as I said, there was a struggle and he—" she gulped air with increasing speed "—took his pleasure of looking and touching."

Pain registered in her eyes, fleeting but obvious even to a guy without much in the way of sensitivity training. He probably shouldn't confuse their strange relationship any more by touching her, but reaching out for her was so natural, so instinctive, he didn't have time to talk himself out of it. He simply folded her in his arms to stop the subtle trembling of her body, to soothe whatever fears he could.

"Jesus, I'm sorry you had to go through that." And how many worse things were women going through today in L.A. as the Guardians stole young women for God only knew what reason?

But he couldn't help those other women right now. He could only reach Linnet and do everything in his power to make sure her misbegotten brothers and fiancé never got their hands on her again.

"It's not frightening when you touch me."

Her words were muffled against his chest as he held her, but Graham heard them all too clearly. The loaded comment called him from his noble intentions and made him consider less honorable ways to chase away Linnet's fears. If touching her helped, he'd be all too pleased to oblige.

The attraction between them had been obvious from the moment he'd wrestled away the dagger she'd pulled on him when she'd found him in the wardrobe. Those intense moments of struggling bodies and heavy breathing had been—well—sexy as hell.

He angled back from her enough to cradle her face in his hand, tipping her chin so that he could meet her eyes. In his mind, he'd been about to tell her he would never harm her.

But somehow, no words issued forth when their gazes locked. Instead, he dipped his head as she arched up on her toes and their lips brushed in a moment of mutual insanity.

But oh, Lord have mercy, it was sweet.

She kissed with an honest-to-God pucker, so soft and sexy that he couldn't resist flicking his tongue along her lower lip, forcing a surprised sigh from her and giving him total access to her mouth. He savored the taste of her—red wine and innocence—even as he told himself to pull away.

She wound her arms around his neck instead, pulling him tighter at the same time her breasts brushed his chest, the peaks cresting into tight points he could feel all too damn well thanks to the wonders of medieval clothing. No combination of spandex, cotton or lace could compete with her naked breasts beneath a layer of velvet and thin linen.

His fingers itched to cup the weight of those soft, full breasts in his hands, but he couldn't take this kiss that far, not after all she'd been through.

He pulled back cold-turkey, the only way he knew to cure an addiction. But even with a few inches separating them, their shared airspace seemed to crackle with sparks they couldn't douse.

"I don't want to confuse the issue." A stupid thing to say, but he'd be lying if he pretended he could think clearly after a kiss like that. "I mean—maybe touching will only complicate this for you when I want to make sure you know I can free that lock and let you go without touching you or leering at you. I'd never restrain you, Linnet. This has to be your decision."

"I feel sort of restrained right now, because what I want to do is kiss you and you won't let me." She took a step closer, her green eyes still clouded with the same heat ruling him.

Professional instincts told him they were approaching this all wrong. He was messing this up royally. But his psych training seemed worlds away in this empty, echoing keep made of stone and wood, a structure that probably didn't even exist in the twenty-first century. Linnet didn't live in a world clogged full of self-help guides for every conceivable emotional problem. Here in a world where the sword ruled and women had few options, maybe he wasn't doing her such a disservice to show her the unselfish ways a man could touch a woman.

Praying he wasn't suffering from a wicked need for justifying his actions, Graham pulled her down to the blanket-covered platform, situating her across his lap. Her green and yellow velvet skirts spilled over his legs and her silky hair fell over his arm, surrounding him in her softness.

"I want to kiss you, too." For about three days straight. Preferably while he buried himself deep inside her. "But I would not replace one bad memory for you with another if you start to panic. Considering the scenario that got you into the belt, I think we'd be wise not to hold each other when I spring you of it. Does that make sense?"

"You fear I will think you are restraining me?" Her hip settled deeper into his lap and he thought he'd jump right out of his skin.

"Bingo." With an effort, he uncrossed his desire-dazed eyes and focused on the matter at hand. "If I keep you here, maybe you will remember you can get up and walk away whenever you want."

He needed to reassure her, to make this right for her, more than he needed to indulge his hunger. Maybe it had just been too long since his ex had taken up with Brendan, because he couldn't remember a time in his life when sex had felt so important. So freaking urgent.

"It's a good idea." She wrapped her arms about his neck again. "I'll hold on to you, but you won't hold on to me. That way I'll remember I'm in charge."

A lesser man might have let out a wolf whistle at the thought of a medieval sexpot declaring herself in charge as she lifted her skirt. But Graham settled for gripping his pocketknife all the more firmly, imprinting the shape of the case into his palm as he fought for some measure of control.

A feat becoming more difficult by the second as Linnet brushed her hem higher and higher up her calves.

Her thighs.

Heat singed his veins at the sight of her and he thought he might combust when he remembered that medieval maidens didn't even own panties. How did men function in a world where virtually every female walked around commando on a day-to-day basis?

But all his sex fantasies evaporated when she lifted

the skirts high enough to expose the delicate metal bands around her hips, curving into a shield that covered her mound and dipped between her thighs.

Perversely, the shield was covered with an etched rose and padlocked with a heart-shaped chunk of metal. Whoever had done this to her was a bastard in the worst sense and Graham promised himself he wouldn't be leaving Linnet's world until he saw the man suffer.

"It is not as bad as it looks," Linnet assured him, making him feel like the world's biggest loser for putting her in the position of making him feel better about a wrong done to her.

"Bullshit." He reached for the heart-shaped lock and tilted the tip of his knife inside the mechanism. "It's worse."

His fingers practically shook with anger as he worked, searching for any latch he might catch with the tip. Failure was not an option.

"Nay." Linnet's hand skimmed his shoulder as he worked, her touch igniting a heat he couldn't afford to feel now. "I did not understand the full import of what the belt caused me to miss until you kissed me, Graham."

His head shot up to search her face, and he found only sincerity and…desire.

"No." He couldn't let her think he was the answer to her problems. She'd have issues with men—with sexuality—for a long time and he needed to respect that. "But you don't have to accept the first man who lights that fire. You could have any man you choose."

Even in L.A., home to thousands of too-good-to-be-true women, Linnet would turn male heads wherever she went.

"You think I would accept any man who kissed me?" Annoyance slashed through her words while her body went rigid.

"I just meant that you don't need to settle for anyone. Not me, not Kendrick, not anyone who doesn't totally rock your world. I'm just saying that maybe the kiss happened because of the circumstances. Sometimes when situations feel intense, a lot of emotions can kick in that you might not normally feel." He worked the lock slowly, searching for the move that would slide it free, but it was no easy task with Linnet's bare legs sprawled out in front of him.

"You think we kissed because I'm on the run from my betrothed and you just happened to be here?" Her incensed tone told him how likely she thought his explanation. Obviously, she was offended. "Tell me, Graham, in your work as a sheriff in your lands, do you kiss every woman in distress?"

Okay, maybe not. Perhaps she had a point. But before he could tell her as much, his blade found the catch inside the lock and sent the arm popping free.

Relief poured through him, making him realize how tense he'd been. She yelped in surprise as she stared down at the metal lock dangling open. The rest of the device still remained hooked, but now that the padlock had come undone, she could unfasten the last of it on her own.

He would have helped if she'd asked him, but she just

continued to stare downward, her long hair shielding her expression until she looked up at him through misty eyes.

"Thank you." Sniffling, she dropped her skirts to cover her unlocked belt, embarrassment seeming to war with the gratitude he saw clearly in her eyes. "I am not happy with your words, but I am in your debt for the service you've done for me."

Rising to her feet, she surprised him by dipping a little girlie bow—a curtsy?—as if to pay him some sort of Old World–style respect. What was he—the Godfather? He felt two inches tall that she would think she had to curtsy to a cop.

"I'm glad I could help. You want me to leave you alone so you can—you know—take off the rest of it for good?"

She must be dying to wrench it loose. But she shook her head and nodded toward the doors and the second-story balcony where they'd entered.

"I need to go somewhere special to take this thing off and free myself, because once it comes unfastened, I'm going to make very sure I never see the dreaded item again."

And without another word, she exited onto the balcony and hefted the wooden plank to her shoulder as if to descend by herself. Little did she know, she didn't have a prayer of going anywhere without him since her brothers could be searching for her even now. The way Graham figured it, unfastening a woman's chastity belt implied a certain amount of obligation in a relationship.

Damned if he didn't have to fall ass-backward nine centuries to make a commitment to a woman—such as it was. But at the very least, he could make sure she remained safe long enough to celebrate her newfound freedom.

6

FINGERS SNAGGING on the rough-hewn plank that would lead her out of the keep, Linnet trembled with the knowledge that she could unfasten her intimate prison as soon as she reached her private place in the forest. She hefted the board and cursed herself for her weakness where Graham was concerned, even if he had saved her from—so much. Still, how could she have allowed herself to kiss a man who thought she would give away her favor so easily?

A splinter tore her skin just as the plank was lifted from her hands and thrust over the balcony to form a steep walkway down to the ground.

"You can leave if you want." Graham stood beside her, glaring down at the grass. "But I'm invested in keeping you safe now, so you can be damn sure that where you go, I go."

"News flash, babe." She tested his phrasing on her tongue and found the strange words to her liking. "I plan to wash away some old fears when I remove this belt you've unlocked and there's a creek not half a league to the west."

"You're going swimming?" His glare didn't diminish as he turned it on her.

"Bathing, actually." Her heart still fluttered wildly in her chest after their kiss. And now, no matter that she was mad at him, she found herself wondering what it might be like to bathe with him.

The thought brought with it a burning need to observe him without his garments.

"You might want to rethink that since I'm serious about going with you." He backed through the open door leading onto the balcony from the bedchamber and retrieved his sword.

"I don't need to rethink anything." She lifted her foot to the plank to begin her descent and willed her toes not to tremble like her suddenly overexcited insides.

"You can't wait another day to wash up? You sure as hell smell clean to me." He reached for her hand, steadying her in spite of his obvious frustration.

"Unfastening a lock might not seem all that important to you, but in my life, this is a tremendous cause for celebration." She itched to take the whole thing off, but hadn't been able to accomplish the task in front of Graham. She'd hopped off his lap before he could undo the full restraint, preferring to remove it in private. Or underneath the water of a fast-rushing stream.

She'd edged down the board far enough where Graham either had to let go or join her.

"Splashing around in a cold-water stream full of rocks and sticks is your idea of a celebration? What you need is a six-pack and a cigar."

He followed her onto the plank as he grumbled, however, and Linnet hoped she hadn't made a mistake by maneuvering him into joining her. But she couldn't remain in the house with him after the awkward encounter they'd shared. His presence made her restless with want of his kiss and his rebuff stung.

She'd hoped maybe the cold sting of the creek water would ease the heat in her veins.

"You owe me a story while we walk," Linnet hopped off the end of the board while Graham edged the rest of the way down. "Remember your promise to reveal your homeland if I allowed you to unlock the latch?"

"Trust me, you'd be just as glad to put that off to another day."

"I would have been just as glad to forestall showing you my steel bonds, but you refused to accept any excuse."

He muttered and cursed but did not argue. Linnet appreciated their activity since it delayed the need to sleep for a little longer. Her dreams waited her there, and she feared their growing urgency—a certain omen of Kendrick's imminent return.

"I live in Los Angeles, California. Long Beach, actually. Don't suppose you've heard of it?" He tugged his sword out of its case as they walked side by side.

"Los Angeles. That is a Moorish land?" Her lack of knowledge frustrated her. "My brothers possess scant education and even fewer books, so I am unfamiliar with this kingdom you speak of."

"I've traveled pretty damn far to be here, so I wouldn't be surprised if L.A. hadn't made it on to a map yet." He swung the sword in an easy arc, the way a warrior did when he readied himself for the practice yard.

His muscles strained against the fabric of his shirt, his arm flexing and stretching to wield the weapon. Linnet found she could not remove her eyes from his impressive form.

"Your home lies to the south, then?" She licked her lips in memory of Graham's kiss and the last time she'd felt his arms about her.

"Not quite."

"The east then?"

He paused in his lightning quick strokes of the blade through the air.

"Sort of. If you go east and keep on going. Far. You'd get to Los Angeles that way." He grinned as if pleased with this answer.

She wanted to question him more about his language and customs, his culture and his people, but he seemed eager to quit the conversation and he *had* given her the basic answer she sought.

"Do you have plans to return?" The notion shouldn't upset her, yet her heart jumped nervously at the idea. But perhaps that was only because she'd shared intriguing conversation with the man.

She didn't want to think about the even more in-triguing kiss. Or the delicious swirl of hunger that seized her whole body, not just her lips.

"I didn't make much of a map on my way here, so I'm not sure I could return home if I tried." He reached with his sword to hack off a branch of wild strawberries trailing over a dead tree stump. "But one of these days I'll have to give it a go."

"Are you ever going to reveal how you came to be in my wardrobe yesterday?" She plucked a berry off the branch he held out to her. Her teeth sank easily into the soft flesh as the juice burst warmly over her tongue.

"That question wasn't part of the deal." He halted his footsteps as they reached the creek. "I'll be damned."

"It's pretty, isn't it?" She paused to admire the view as well. "I'd forgotten how beautiful it was."

A clear stream tripped over rocks at one side of the clearing to fall down a short hill in a misty cascade of water. The water was deeper at the basin of the falls, providing a pool perfect for bathing.

Apparently Graham thought the same thing, since he placed his sword on a rock and began to unfasten his shirt.

"What are you doing?"

"I thought we were here to bathe." Shrugging out of his shirt, he reached for the placket of his braies.

"*I'm* here to bathe." She thought she should probably protest his imminent nakedness, but the image of his muscular chest resembled a dream vision she'd had long ago, shortly after Kendrick had clamped her into the belt.

The vivid memory rattled her, tying her tongue as she struggled to recall pieces of that long-ago dream that didn't involve torrid lovemaking and wanton sexuality.

"Oh my God." Her words yelped from her throat.

"Too much for you?" Graham winked as he paused

in unfastening his pants. "You could always just turn around."

"It's not that." Well, partially it was that. In her dream memory, his manhood had been most impressive and incredibly...pleasurable. "I just had the unsettling sensation that we've been here before."

"What do you mean?" Frowning, he kicked off his strange leather shoes with unusual lacings.

She debated how much to tell him since her visions had caused trouble for her in the past—mostly with her family, but once with a nobleman who'd stopped at Welborne Keep for a meal. Linnet had been struck by the image of him killing his wife as he calmly devoured a meal of roast pheasant, and she'd insisted that he leave. Her family had been as furious as the nobleman, but he'd departed during the night without a word.

His wife's body had been found some weeks later by a pack of hunting hounds, only making her family more angry with her.

"I have visions sometimes. My mother called it the Sight but I do not think the images I see are always accurate." She tried to shrug off the moment now that she'd attracted too much attention to her odd waking dreams. "Seeing you prepare to bathe made me remember a vision I had long ago."

"You were dreaming about me before I even arrived. I call that a good sign." His easy grin returned and Linnet counted her blessings he had not accused her of prophecy or any of the other, more hateful things her brothers had in the past.

Still, the details of the dream she'd had a few short years ago continued to plague her as she turned her back so he could undress. The memories taunted her with seductive snippets of what it felt like to be in Graham's arms, to kiss his naked, wet skin with lustful hunger. To seat herself on his lap in the water and spread her legs wide for him. To open herself to him completely and rid herself of the innocence Kendrick coveted for his own.

What if that long ago dream—the one that had taken place beside this very creek—was a premonition? The notion created a sudden, unbearable ache between her thighs. Could fate have conspired to put Graham Lawson in her reach on the very day she could finally reclaim her own body?

The feelings he inspired in her suddenly felt less intimidating and more fated. Graham had already been the key to unlocking her future—and not just because he was handy with a pocketknife.

And hadn't her visions of a hazy mystery stranger come to her more often lately? That could be a sign as well. As the warmth between her thighs became more insistent, she was seized with a powerful understanding of what she needed to do next.

As she heard the sound of Graham walking into the water, she turned around slowly again, ready to face what happened next in her dream—what she now knew should happen in reality.

The best way to celebrate her freedom from the cursed chastity belt would be to finally make use of the womanhood it had been shielding for so long. Today, right here by this very stream, she would embrace her desires in spite of her betrothed and give her virginity to Graham Lawson.

A MAN KNEW WHEN A WOMAN had something on her mind. He might not have any idea what she was thinking, but there was a definite air to a scheming woman. Graham hadn't recognized the knowing smile when his ex-girlfriend had sweetly asked him to help out with the sword sequence on the movie set where she'd served as an extra. But he damn well knew the smile by now and Linnet Welborne had it.

She didn't even give him any warning when she slipped her overdress—a surcoat, she called it—over her head. In her world, wasn't that halfway home to naked?

"You could have warned me," he called to her as he dutifully turned his back, the image of her undressing imprinted on his brain and making him throb despite the water temperature.

"But you already treated yourself to the view when you hid in my wardrobe," she countered from the bank of the creek. "Or when you unlocked the belt. What would be the point in pretending false modesty now?"

The sentiment sounded downright dangerous to his ears. A beautiful, sex-starved woman who'd been denied all physical pleasure for three years made a point of telling him she wasn't worried about her modesty. The cold water of the creek didn't begin to douse the heat simmering in his veins.

"On the contrary, your modesty is totally called for because I really didn't see much of anything." He'd been a gentleman. Well, at least when he'd picked the lock for her, he'd been super respectful. He probably couldn't say the same about his open ogling when he'd wound up in her bedroom.

But now he would not turn around until he knew she was in the water, her body safely hidden from view. He'd tortured himself enough earlier with superhuman restraint when he'd wrested her from her intimate prison. Speaking of which…

"Do you need any help ditching the rest of that belt?"

He asked out of polite concern, of course. He did not need any more temptation today.

"See for yourself." Behind him, he heard the water splash as she apparently waded into the water.

"Is it—safe?" His imagination already painted a hell of a picture of her naked. The last thing he needed was to see the real deal and remove all doubt about how good she looked without clothes.

"Depends what you consider safe." Her voice emanated from much too close. A few feet behind him, maybe. Her quiet strokes must have moved her quickly through the water to have covered that much distance already.

"Anything involving me naked while you're in the water is probably not a good idea." He turned around carefully, water reaching to the middle of his chest.

She held a bar of soap in one hand and the chastity belt in the other, the skinny silver shackle looking way too small to fit around any woman, let alone a tall teenager who might not have been done growing at the time. Compassion for her—for what this moment must mean for her—helped him put his libido in check for a few minutes at least. Thankfully, she hadn't quite removed all her clothing since a wet, sleeveless garment clung to her shoulders while her breasts remained— praise God—underwater.

He promised himself he wouldn't strain his eyes to see beneath the murky surface, but he had to admit, he was tempted.

"I'm free." Her brow furrowed as if she was still trying to grasp the magnitude of the words. "That miserable, selfish bastard can no longer rule me from afar. I am free."

Before he could comment on her newfound liberty, she folded her arm across her body and flung the chastity belt like a Frisbee before she watched it flip end over silver end through the air then land in the water to float downstream. Away from her.

He turned his attention back to her and found her stalking closer, her bar of soap extended in one hand like Eve with a fateful offering.

"Congratulations." He plucked the soap from her hands and told himself a man couldn't expect more from himself than even Adam had been able to offer.

And Graham was willing to bet a fig leaf hadn't been nearly as alluring as the hint of cleavage through thin, wet linen plastered to Linnet's body now.

Holy hell, he could see beneath the water. Only a

eunuch wouldn't have at least tried to catch a glimpse of those incredible breasts.

"Do you want me to help?" She nodded meaningfully at the soap in his hands.

"With taking a bath?" He couldn't have spluttered more if she'd dunked him for a few minutes. "I'm pretty sure I'll manage."

"In my land, it is a custom for visiting guests to be bathed by their hostess." She floated closer, the ripple from the movement splashing against his chest. She could have stood if she chose, the water barely reaching his shoulders. But she seemed to relish the feel of the water, ducking under wherever possible.

How could she bring those breasts closer? Didn't she know his hands would only obey his brain for so long?

"That sounds like a really dangerous habit for a young woman." Once she touched him, he wouldn't be able to protest anymore.

"Not for me. Not for the past three years." She trod water in front of him while his feet remained planted. "Even if my brothers had called on me to honor that tradition in our home, no man could have taken advantage of me thanks to that cursed shield I wore."

"Then you need to be all the more careful now that you're unprotected in that way." The thought of her putting her hands on some faceless, dirty medieval dude really pissed him off. "What the hell kind of custom is that anyhow?"

She reached for the soap slowly, as if half expecting

him not to give it back. "It is a custom I've always detested until now. You are far more welcome in my tub than any of my brothers' folly-fallen friends."

Sunlight shone through the leaves bent over the creek, casting Linnet in an unearthly glow. The ends of her hair floated in the water around her like a seductive mermaid. The falls crashed into the pool behind him, the sound drowning out the rest of the world as if nothing else mattered but what happened here. Now.

He'd do well to remember that wasn't the case. He needed to remain watchful. Vigilant.

"Is that all you want? To touch each other and discover some of the pleasure you've been missing these past few years?" He could touch her. Introduce her to the delights of her own body even if he couldn't indulge himself as thoroughly as he wanted.

Virginity wasn't a bother or a burden in the Middle Ages, or at least according to the snippet of the exhibit he'd seen in the Sex Through the Ages presentation it wasn't. Her virginal status would be important to whoever she did marry one day.

The bastard. Even if she found some great guy, Graham decided he already hated him.

But there were ways Graham could touch her that wouldn't rob her of that marital prize....

"No. I want to do more than discover *some* of the pleasures. I want to celebrate my freedom by discovering them all." She licked her lower lip before she rushed on. "And you are the man I want to discover them with."

From under the water, he felt her hand graze his chest before brushing lower. Much lower.

And no matter that he had no business touching her, Graham knew he didn't have a prayer of denying her.

"YOU RISK A HELL OF A LOT to be with me." Graham's warning didn't halt her hand's downward trek. She'd set the soap on the creek bank so that she might graze his hip with her bare hands. She marveled at the muscle of his buttock, the warmth of his skin despite the cool water.

"No more risk than you take to be with me." Kendrick would kill this man if he ever found out of her faithlessness, but Linnet vowed he would never learn the truth.

This time alone with Graham soothed what had been long raw inside her and she would repay his kindness by protecting his identity at all costs.

"I have the feeling that our risks will be well rewarded." His arm speared through the water to wrap around her waist and draw her close.

Her heart slapped against her chest so hard she wondered why the reverberation did not make ripples through the water. How brazen she was that her first real embrace with a man would find her almost naked, her chemise soaked to her skin in a transparent veil.

He looked at her intently, as if he could pick her thoughts right out of her head with his dark, brooding stare. His hand fisted in the material of her wet chemise while the creek flowed in a steady rush around their legs. Every sensation—the cold water, his warm hands, the silken flow of the current—seemed all the more intensified to her body's long-denied sensual response. Even the ripple of her chemise between her thighs felt like a lover's caress. A very naughty and delicious touch.

"I seem to grow drunk on feeling," she whispered, swaying on her feet as he brushed a kiss along her shoulder then nudged aside the chemise to expose her bare skin.

"I'm halfway to intoxicated myself." His free hand plunged beneath the surface to find her hem and lift the thin fabric, peeling it away from her body as he undressed her.

A low moan escaped her throat as the stream rushed over her bare breasts, swirling decadently in the valley between them and coaxing her nipples into aching crests. Flinging her chemise onto the bank of the creek, Graham lowered his mouth to circle one tight peak. The wet heat of his lips sent a bolt of lightning crackling through her senses, setting her whole body on fire in answer. Her back arched of its own volition, conspiring to get her as close to the source of that heat as possible.

"More." She wound her fingers through his damp hair and held him closer, delighting in the decadence of his touch.

He obliged her by closing his mouth over the other breast while wrapping her legs around his waist. Just like her dream vision, the feel of his skin against her most private places sent ribbons of pleasure unwinding in her limbs. Her thighs trembled at the contact, and then her whole body began to quiver with a sudden desperation to be possessed. Thoroughly. Completely. Now.

"I want to take you somewhere private." He lifted his head to survey the land, his hair even darker now that it was wet. "Somewhere we can stay for hours—days—without being interrupted."

"I like it here." Her vision of them together had taken place on the grassy creek bank. "I have been imprisoned long enough that I like the idea of being out in the open with the sun at our backs and the fish as our witnesses."

Grinning, he drew her close again. "That's not a fish you're feeling."

He leaned in to kiss her, to take her mouth with slow, deliberate strokes of his tongue. She opened to him, winding her arms about his neck and pressing herself to him as closely as she could. His manhood throbbed against the swollen lips of her nether regions, her sensitive places slick with her own want.

She lifted herself up to take him, ready and eager to experience the earthly delights another man had tried to deny her, but Graham's hands held her hips in place, refusing to let her take that next step.

"I have protection, but I don't think it's as effective if you use it in the water."

"Protection from what?" Confused, she steadied herself on his lap, clutching one broad shoulder for support. "This strikes me as a rather inopportune time to discuss weaponry. Unless of course, you wish to converse about the merits of one sword in particular."

She moved meaningfully against his shaft for emphasis.

"While that would be a mighty damn interesting conversation, I meant I have a way to protect you from getting pregnant, but the device is on the shore along with my clothes."

"What wizardry is this?" She knew that some wise women were rumored to have such potions, but she never would have suspected Graham would possess something that many would deem unnatural.

"No wizardry here. But I promised to keep you safe and that's exactly what I'm going to do."

Without warning, he hefted her out of the water, his strong arms cradling her in a tight grip as he waded to shore. The feel of his chest against the side of her breast reminded her how much she wanted to finish what they'd started.

No sooner had he gathered up their clothes than a rustling sound emanated from the undergrowth nearby. She might have called to whatever bird or animal lurked there, but he wrenched her away from that patch of forest with an ironclad grip.

Stifling her yelp with his hand, he shoved them behind a thick tree and pressed her against the bark, shielding her with his body as the thunder of approaching hooves pounded the ground all around them. Her skin still flaming from his touch, she could scarcely appreciate the feel of him against her since the oncoming riders bore a bloodred standard she recognized all too well.

Saints preserve them, her betrothed had returned from the Holy Lands to claim her.

7

THERE WAS A TIME in Graham's life where he would have been hard-pressed to imagine any scenario involving getting naked with a woman that wouldn't put a smile on his face. But then, he'd never pictured himself as the kind of guy stupid enough to get carried away with a female he'd essentially stolen from her own home.

He didn't breathe for the endless seconds that six horses galloped into view, mouths foaming from overwork. Wrapping both arms around Linnet to keep her still, he didn't care about arming himself now when a glint of silver could attract unwanted attention. Bad enough they were naked in the woods, their bare butts an easy target for anyone looking their way, although thankfully their hiding place probably sat some fifty yards from the matted grass that must serve as a rarely traveled road.

Graham had outwitted Linnet's three brothers with a little ingenuity, but he'd never be able to take down six guys on horseback when he didn't have so much as a pair of jockey shorts to use as a shield and he had Linnet to protect.

A hell of a time for a hard-on.

The third knight raced by their tree neck-and-neck with a fourth, raising dust and clods of fresh soil as they jounced around on the biggest horses Graham had ever seen. Definitely not thoroughbreds, the animals looked handpicked for size, their breadth coming closer to Clydesdales than racing stock.

"'Tis him. My betrothed," Linnet whispered as the fifth man entered their field of vision. She trembled so much in his arms he half feared she'd shiver right out of his grasp. He held her tighter to reassure her, but that surely didn't help his—ah—condition.

The man she pointed out rode his stallion like some guys rode their motorcycles—bent low over the neck as if he savored every millisecond of speed he gained with the decreased wind resistance. But this was no thrill seeker who relished the joy of the wind in his hair. The man's intense expression and hollowed eyes gave him the appearance of a zealot more than a warrior. Despite the chain mail and the decorative banner featuring a bear on a red field, Burke Kendrick looked nothing like a patron of knightly chivalry. Maybe Graham was letting his protectiveness for Linnet do his seeing for him, but he could swear Kendrick shared the same glare in his eyes as the guys hanging out on death row. The dudes with nothing to lose because they'd already committed the worst of crimes.

Only when the last horse had raced past the tree where they hid did Graham realize he'd taken little note of Kendrick's physical features. But then, he wouldn't be giving the jerk's description to a police sketch artist, so he figured it was more important to record a personal impression of the man than to post an APB via the town crier.

"What will we do?" Linnet's shaky words forced him to brush off his thoughts and focus on their situation.

"Do you believe they had six overheated animals and didn't even bat an eye when they passed a water source?" How could he focus when he had so much to process? He was a damn good cop in the world where he knew how to obtain backup, where to dig for more information on a case and how twenty-first century criminals behaved.

But here—wherever here was—he was way the hell off his game.

"They're obviously in a hurry."

"In too much of a hurry to stop at your brother's house—er, uh, castle?"

"I don't think Kendrick would even realize that holding belonged to my family. He doesn't know all that much about the Welbornes."

An interesting state of affairs he'd have to question her about, right after he willed away the hunger for her that still gnawed at him in spite of everything.

"Where do you think he's headed in such an all-fired hurry?" He eased away from her with regret and handed her the rumpled mass of her dresses that he'd snatched off the ground as a precaution when he'd heard riders.

"To claim me for his bride." She slid into the yellow under-dress and he mourned the loss of the most gorgeous visual of a woman he'd ever seen.

"Do you realize how lucky we were to have left Welborne Keep when we did?" For the first time, he wondered if he'd had some greater purpose to achieve by coming here. Not only would he find the clue to understanding the Guardians, but maybe he was meant to be here in order to save Linnet from far more harm than marital woes and a quickie divorce.

Now that he'd seen Kendrick for himself, he better understood her need to run.

"I know we are fortunate. *I* am fortunate. I saw in my mind's eye that Kendrick approached. 'Twas why I've scarcely slept the past week. The dreams kept growing more and more frightening. His face became more and more clear." She picked a leaf out of her hair before securing a thin braid in a loop around the back of her head. Her unsteady fingers as she worked proved how unsettling the dreams must have been.

Graham buttoned his fly and tucked in his shirt before moving to help Linnet with her laces. The weather had been temperate, but as the day grew late, the warm summer day cooled slightly.

"What is it with you and the visions?" He remembered her talking about her dreams before as if they meant more than an excuse to keep hitting the snooze alarm.

"I have the Sight." She looked proud of the fact for all of two seconds before her face fell. "But it has become a fearsome burden since the revelation of my future became filled with images of knives and blood and—"

"Holy shit." He released the last of her dress's laces

and smacked his forehead as his thoughts started to unjumble and make sense. "Parapsychology."

"Is this another one of your foreign words?" Her brow furrowed with impatience. Or worry.

"Two women were kidnapped at a local—that is—a place in my homeland recently and they had taken interest in phenomena like the Sight." The pair of students had been attending a parapsychology workshop on campus. And Linnet had some kind of precognition abilities.

When his answer didn't seem to have clarified matters for her, he explained what he could in the hope she'd help him figure out whatever it was he'd come here to learn.

"I'm trying to help those missing women and I have reason to believe they were taken by men who bore the same symbols as the carving on your—uh—"

"The carving you were so interested in." She completed his thought diplomatically, her cheeks coloring. "It's interesting you mention the Sight because I believe that was one of the reasons Kendrick wanted to marry me."

Graham went still, hand braced on a tree trunk already putting a barrier between her and the bad guys. The significance of her admission turned his cop thoughts to high speed.

"What do you mean?" He'd worry about getting them back to the fortification in one piece in a little while. Preferably after dark. For now, he had all the time in the world to listen to whatever Linnet had to say.

He just needed to keep his hands off her long enough to keep his brain engaged.

"DON'T YOU THINK WE SHOULD make haste and return to the security of my brother's holding?" Linnet could not suppress her shivers now that her worst fears had been confirmed.

She understood that Graham could keep her safe. Seeing the way his whole manner had changed at the first sign of trouble helped her realize that he was far more accomplished a warrior than she knew. He'd pinned her to that black mulberry tree with nothing but a sword to protect her, his reactions lightning swift to danger. But even though she'd recognized Graham's prowess, she also knew he was not hers to command. He'd helped her escape her family seat, but he was a stranger to her lands, a visitor who would one day leave her to fend for herself.

"We're not going anywhere until it's dark. Too dangerous." He gestured toward the waterfall at the mouth of the creek. "Let's use the water as a shield for our movements. We can settle in behind the falls until the sun sets."

She hesitated only a moment, making a decision to have still more faith in the man who hid her from Burke Kendrick. Graham was not a brute in the fashion of her brothers. Besides, she'd dreamed favorably of him. She would trust him, as she trusted in her visions.

Following him through the labyrinth of undergrowth and low-hanging branches, Linnet trudged behind him toward the place he indicated. She could not look at the creek without remembering what they had nearly shared in those murky depths.

As soon as they reached a spot hidden from view where the riders had passed, Graham pivoted to face her.

"Why do you think the swine wanted to wed you because of the Sight?" Removing his sword from its case, he laid out the leather satchel as a makeshift seat and waved her toward it.

She noticed he kept his weapon close to his hand as he sat beside her beneath a throng of ash and elder trees. They faced the waterfall so they could see the pathway through the water and the spray that emanated from it. A wave of fatigue hit her as she settled her skirts around her legs. No surprise since she hadn't slept the night before and the day was already growing old. Still, because the year had nearly turned to Midsummer, daylight would linger a few more hours.

"I don't know *why* he was interested in my gift, but I am certain that he sought me out because of it." She had not thought about the past in so long, the memories never pleasant. But they came to her easily enough as she sat beside Graham, his legs sprawled out in front of him, strong thighs stretching his blue braies wrought of the most interesting fabric she'd ever seen.

"You're tired." He did not need to ask since her head had somehow tipped onto his shoulder while she'd been thinking.

She lifted it in surprise now, but he only shifted her closer and wrapped his arm about her waist. Perhaps he simply did it to keep the rest of her upright, but that didn't prevent her from enjoying the warm male strength of him banded about her waist.

"Sorry." Heat rolled through her in spite of her exhaustion, desire for this man still very much alive. But first, she needed to tell him about her betrothal. "I heard about Kendrick before I met him. First from a traveler who spent a night at Welborne Keep and then later from my brothers, who had met Kendrick when he came searching for the woman who'd impressed that first traveler."

She toyed with a stone on the ground beside her, the small pebble no doubt smoothed by years of water rushing over it when the creek rose high.

"Rumors of your skill at bathing strange men had spread?" He pulled her legs into his lap, his one hand disappearing under her skirt.

"Hardly." She delighted in the slow ascension of his fingers up her calf, behind her knee, swirling in the hollow there. "Although I am willing to test my bathing skills on you again as soon as you think it safe."

He pushed her hem farther up her legs, the action stirring a slight breeze against her thighs and—*ooh*— beyond. The sensation made her squirm with want until she nearly dropped the stone she still clenched in one hand.

"We will test the water again soon enough." He tightened his grip about her waist, as if steadying her for the trek of his fingers down the inside of her thigh. "But first tell me what impressed the first traveler that spurred Kendrick's interest."

Her pulse quickened as he traced a path to the outside of her leg to palm one hip.

"I had a vision of the man's wife—dead. I knew as surely as I breathed that he had killed her, even though he talked about her as if she still sat at home waiting for his return." The vision had been ugly and vivid, violent moments between a husband and wife that outside eyes wouldn't normally ever see. "I told my kin, but they only laughed and shared my 'foolish fears' with the man himself. He looked at me strangely after that and left in all haste during the night."

Graham's hand halted, his forehead tipping against hers as he held her.

"You are sure this event you saw actually happened?"

"I do not think I saw the future that time. I believe that vision was in the past, although I have had dreams that have foretold events yet to come. But yes, I know the vision was true since the unfortunate woman's body was found a fortnight later."

She shivered in spite of the warmth of his body next to hers, her knuckles white around the stone she hadn't realized she'd held in a death grip as she spoke.

"And Kendrick got off on that," Graham mused to himself in his strange dialect that she understood more by his tone of voice than his words.

"He queried me greatly about my visions when he found me—again, thanks to my brothers who cannot see beyond their own coffers." She pitched the stone into the waterfall with a forceful toss. If only she could be rid of her kinsmen as easily.

"But he does not have you anymore." Graham

pulled her farther onto his lap, displacing more of her skirts until half her thighs were exposed to the muted daylight and gentle breeze. "I think I should have you instead."

Linnet lifted her gaze to meet his and found his expression fierce. Possessive. His aspect inflamed her, tempted her to forget that he was a foreigner with secrets and a life that didn't include her. Just now, she could only care that he was a man. A strong, intelligent and honorable man.

And she, for her part, remained an aching woman who had been too long deprived.

Graham might leave her tomorrow for a woman in his homeland, or he could simply vanish from her life as startlingly as he had entered it. She'd be a folly-fallen fool to allow this moment with him to pass through her fingers.

Arching against him, she gave herself to the moment. The man. She only had one condition, and she whispered it in his ear.

"Show me everything."

TALK ABOUT RISING to a challenge.

Graham figured if he rose any higher he'd be lightheaded for a week. As it was, he strained his fly like the superhero who burst out of clothes, leaving only rags behind.

Linnet's lips brushed his cheek as she whispered her innocent command in his ear, her tongue darting out to taste him.

"You don't want much, do you?" He stroked the

silky skin of her hip, hoping he could take his time to give her the slow build she deserved after how long she'd waited to be touched.

"I trust you to give me what I want." She edged closer to him on the leather satchel, her legs thrown over his in a sprawl of soft feminine flesh.

He brought his mouth down to hers, ready for another taste, needing that sweet flavor on his lips to help tide him over until he undressed her. He'd tied the laces on her outer gown before, but he had no clue what to do with the rest of it and a man damn well ought to be able to undress a woman.

Tunneling his hand under her long hair, he found her neck and tilted her head for better access. The soft sigh in the back of her throat spoke volumes.

A light breeze blew over the water and covered them with a fine mist from the waterfall but it did nothing to cool the rising heat between them. Graham never wanted to stop touching her, her responsive wriggles and moans making him crazy.

Shoving aside her skirts the rest of the way, he exposed her to the summer wind and the waterfall spray. Judging from the way she squealed, her cheeks flushed, he supposed she appreciated the sensation after the shield had covered her for so long.

His fingers worked the laces on her gown, one after another in a seemingly endless row up her side. He started at her hip and worked toward her breast, lingering over the last tie to cop a feel of her softness. He could see the shape of her through the fabric of her dress, the green velvet starting to fall from her shoulders the more he loosened the ties. With nothing but the yellow linen to cover her, her nipples pressed eagerly at the material.

Distracted by the sight, he bent to test the feel of them between his lips. Against his tongue. The pebbled tips trembled against his mouth while he untied the laces on her other side. Her breasts were so beautiful. So full and soft and high.

And the rest of her...

He released her breasts just long enough to tug the loosened garments over her head, unveiling all of her to his gaze.

"What a sin to hide you away." He tried not to let the anger out now when he needed to be sensitive to her and what she'd been through.

But when he unleashed the fury on the target most deserving...

"You need to see this." He lifted her to her feet, a perfect wood nymph with pale skin and huge, luminous eyes.

Carrying her over to the water's edge, he found the small pool that was relatively undisturbed. At least, he could see his reflection in the water. He stood her at the edge and positioned himself behind her, his arms wrapped around her waist.

"Look at you." He could hardly believe his own eyes looking down at the reflection of them together.

She could have been Lady Godiva, since her hair was so long she could have ridden around town with enough to cover all her secret places. Graham brushed it away from her shoulders, his skin bronzed and tawny next to her creamy flesh.

A small gasp escaped her lips as she stared down as if mesmerized.

"I am free." Her hand followed the line of her belly from one hip bone to the other, tracing the faint but definite crease on her skin where the belt she'd once worn had rested.

"You damn well are." He covered her hand with his, his fingers joining hers in their thoughtful trek, and he felt her sharp intake of breath at the sensation.

She was a virgin.

He could hardly wrap his head around that. The thought that no one else had ever shown her pleasure before had already made him angry on her behalf.

Now, he felt only a determination to make up for every lost second. Not necessarily all today, since he had a little more sensitivity for her first time than that. But sooner or later, he intended to show her everything she'd been missing with whatever time they might have together, just as she'd asked.

It would be his pleasure to touch her more. To taste her more. To discover what made her shudder with fulfillment.

Nipping her shoulder with his teeth, he licked his way up her neck and inhaled her clean fragrance, never taking his attention off her tantalizing reflection in the water, even when her eyes fell closed.

"I've been fantasizing about doing this ever since I

watched you undress for bed. Open your eyes, Linnet." He hooked his foot around her ankle and coaxed her leg wide. "I want you to see everything that I see."

8

HER REFLECTION IN THE SMALL inlet behind the waterfall bore little resemblance to the woman she knew from her looking glass.

This woman's eyes were not wary and alert, but languid and knowing. Her lips lacked the thin, pursed quality they had taken on in recent years, and now swelled with moist ripeness. Her hair tripped wildly over her shoulders, wind-tossed and unruly, barely cloaking her body like a seductive veil.

He had done this to her. A man.

"This is how it should be between a man and a woman." She liked the stranger in the reflection, the bold, brazen wench who did not run from life but embraced it with open arms.

And, saints preserve her, open legs.

"'Tis wicked and wonderful at the same time," she murmured, lifting her arm to encircle his head.

Their gazes met, held, in the water.

"Sweetheart, trust me, it's all good." He cupped her breasts with strong, broad hands, testing their weight, outlining their shape. The sight of his fingers on her pale skin made her knees weak.

Fortunately he shifted his stance to plant his thigh between her legs, his hard male strength holding her up when she would have pooled at his feet. And yet, that position provided no relief from the heat building within her. Her most private places met the taut muscle of his thigh, making her shudder with pleasure and tremble for more.

His hands started their slow descent from her breasts, tracking down her sides with deliberate thoroughness. Fire leaped within her at his touch, the flames licking her skin and traveling south far faster than his slowly moving palms.

The fall of water filled her ears with its dull roar, a noise she would never forget as long as she lived. Graham filled her other senses and she realized she wanted him to fill *her* with a desperation that bordered on madness.

She stifled a low whimper as his hand reached the pale curls that were her only shield from him now that her metal prison was long gone.

"You like that?" He wound one silken tendril around his finger while he waited for her reply.

She caught herself nodding frantically in the liquid mirror and then stopped herself.

"Yes." It felt good to speak the word aloud, to claim her own pleasure. "Very much."

"Don't be afraid to tell me what you want." He parted the swollen folds of her sex and slid two fingers along the damp seam.

She cried out with the surprising rush of pure bliss that followed, so intense it contracted like a fist in her womb.

"This." Her breath seemed to have been sucked from her lungs, leaving her gasping for any sign of air. "I enjoy this."

She held the rest of her body perfectly still, her full attention devoted to the intensely sensual feel of his finger playing in her wetness, teasing her with her slick response.

"I like this, too." He gave her sex a soft pinch between his thumb and forefinger, then circled her nipple with his other hand. "And this."

As if he'd somehow drawn a physical connection from one place to another, a line of flames erupted between them. The sensations heightened, singeing her insides and making her wonder what would happen to all that heat. She felt it building, building, and didn't know where she could put it all. The vision in the pond blurred as her eyes ceased to focus, her response to Graham's touches growing more out of control and wild and—

Ooh. Her cry drowned out the noise of the waterfall as a wave of pleasure ripped through her so strongly she would have fallen if Graham's leg hadn't been there to keep her standing.

The heavens seemed to erupt with shooting stars behind her eyes as one wave of fulfillment after another rocked her body. Her womb pulsed with joyous convulsions, the feeling a delicious revelation to her after years of total denial.

She couldn't speak, couldn't think, and she could scarcely move as the angels above broke into spontaneous, blissful chorus at her good fortune in discover-

ing what a man could do for a woman if he had any
interest in pleasing her.

Finally, she gave up chasing her breath, resigned to
waiting for it to return. Her heart hammered reck-
lessly inside her chest as the last spasms of pleasure
made her twitch. Graham turned her in his arms,
spinning her to face him.

"That had to be the most erotic thing I've ever seen."
He kissed her hard, the thrust of his tongue against hers
reminding her that he hadn't reached the same fulfillment as he'd given her.

He must still be waiting. Wanting.

Poor man.

Unsure how to proceed, she let instinct guide her,
shutting out the guilty voice inside her head that chas-
tised her for not returning the fulfillment he'd given her.
Instead, she followed the movements of his tongue with
her own, taking note of the seductive mating of mouths.

No. That couldn't be enough. Not after all he'd done
for her. He'd freed her in so many ways, but this last was
the most delightful.

Pulling away, she met his gaze in the amber rays of
sunset, admiring the way the light found hints of russet
in his dark hair. She touched one of those burnished
patches with her fingers, surprised at the silken feel of
his straight hair, her own already curling from their
swim earlier.

"I wish to make you feel the way I did just now." She
splayed her hands on his chest to keep him at arm's
length since she did not want him to distract her with

kisses that would make her forget her noble purpose. "Show me how to give that to you."

"Honey, you deliver just by breathing." He tried to lean in for another kiss, but she stopped him with a hand pressed to his chest.

"I do not understand." She shivered as a gust of breeze blew a spray of water on her bare shoulders, her skin sensitized for the slightest touch. "If you felt the way I do, your knees would be shaking and your whole body would convulse with lush spasms."

"You don't want to see me start convulsing yet. Trust me on that." He backed a step and looked out over the water. "Come under the waterfall with me and I promise I'll be shaking like there's no tomorrow before you can say 'dream come true.'"

She didn't ask why she would say such a thing in the middle of passionate embraces. She simply took his hand and followed him into the shallow inlet alongside the waterfall, their reflections faded now as the day's shadows grew long.

The cool water reached her ankles for several steps before it deepened to splash lightly against her knees. When they arrived at the waterfall, Graham stepped behind it and drew her behind the curtain of water with him, the cocoon of natural sounds and misty spray sheltering them from the rest of the world.

The soft glimmer of twilight cast Graham's body in detailed relief, outlining his powerful arms and broad chest for her viewing pleasure. His blue eyes invited her closer, luring her as surely as the hand he extended to her.

Taking it without question, she was rewarded by his quiet words of instruction.

"Touch me."

She didn't have to ask where he would like to be touched. She might be a virgin, but she knew well enough what the heat in a man's gaze meant.

Reaching out, she ran her fingertip from the base of him to the thick head, following the line of one pulsing vein for a map. The heat of him throbbed against her hand and she wondered how such velvety skin could contain a staff so rock hard.

A shudder ripped through his body as she held him, the small movement letting her know how much her touch affected him. But could she really accomplish a task so astonishing as he'd managed for her on the shore?

Tantalized by the thought, she pressed a kiss to his chest and found new courage in the urgent hammer of his heart against her lips. Licking the solid wall of muscle, she discovered she liked his musky male taste. Hands splayed on his chest, she kept enough distance from him to prevent herself from rubbing her whole body against him and losing herself in the sultry heaven she knew he could provide.

Tasting her way down his chest, he let out a low groan when she bent to her knees in the water, water surging to her shoulders. Had he suspected her motives? She cupped the base of him in her hands and lowered her mouth to test the flavor of the dark, glistening head, her tongue running tentatively around the rim.

She noted Graham's reaction with interest, his whole

body growing even more rigid in ways she hadn't dreamed possible at this point. Encouraged, she braced her hands on his thighs and lowered her mouth around him. His muscles clenched beneath her palms, his fingers sifting restlessly through her hair.

The taste of him pleased her, aroused her, the seductive motion imitating the sex act she craved with him. She wanted to suggest it, but he was already hauling her up out of the water, pushing her back toward the spray of the cascading stream.

"You're too damn good to be true." He spun them around so that he backed into the falls instead of her, allowing her to decide if she wanted to duck under with him or not. "I'm going to sob like a little girl if I wake up and find out this was only a dream."

Smiling, she entered the downpour with him, the water only rising to their knees here where the rocks rose a bit higher beneath their feet.

"Dreams do not feel this good." The cold water fell with pounding force on her shoulders and back, causing her skin to tighten with the chill for a moment before the pleasure of the rivulets sliding over her bare skin warmed her again.

"I need to cool off before I lose it." He tipped his head back to take the deluge on his face. "I didn't bring protection into the water with me."

"You don't need a sword with me," she whispered in his ear as she gently gripped his shaft in her hand, surprised at her own boldness.

She had no intention of allowing him to cool off. Not

when she had chosen him to initiate her into womanhood. Her need seemed far more important than arming himself or protecting her, or whatever he meant by forgetting protection.

He hauled her close with one arm, her breasts flattening against his chest. With his free hand, he returned the same pleasure she gave him, his fingers sliding between her legs to cup her mound. The pleasure was instant; as if she hadn't already experienced the keen delight he'd given her earlier. Then his fingers moved, performing a slow massage of painstakingly deliberate circles and it suddenly required all of her concentration and tremendous effort just to continue touching him when she wanted nothing more than to experience that wave of magic he could make.

"You are much more skilled at this than me." She panted the words over her building passion, scarcely able to articulate her thoughts. "You must wait so I can catch up with pleasuring you."

"Sexual handicapping. I love it." His words confused her, as always, but she did not question, could not care what his foreign expressions might mean.

"Never mind catching up. I want to feel you inside me." She leaned out of the torrent of water to make sure he heard her.

The time had come to breach her maidenhead, and she wanted this man to do it. Not some cold, impersonal device crafted by Kendrick for initiating a woman. She wanted to feel the heat, the velvety strength of Graham's manhood between her legs.

"It isn't safe." He stepped out of the downpour as well, his eyes dark and glittering in the shadowy cave of rock and water with naught but a wavering shaft of moonlight to illuminate them.

"No one can see us." She traced the strong line of his jaw, the dark bristly shadow giving him a dangerous aspect. "And I am very ready for you."

She could feel her heartbeat throb between her thighs, her sex wet with readiness. She had to have him.

Now.

"Are you sure?"

Graham gritted his teeth against the need for her, knowing he was an idiot even to consider taking her. But it had to be a dream. A long as hell dream. Or maybe he'd cracked his head open back at the J. Paul Getty Museum and even now he was bleeding out on a sleek marble floor somewhere and what he was feeling was all part of his dying last wish.

And hot damn, but this was the way to go.

"I'm very sure." Linnet stroked him in sporadic bursts of frenzied touches, her green eyes dazed and heavy-lidded with desire as she swayed on her feet in the water.

"Then we do this my way." He hadn't ever tried the pull-out method, knowing it was a dumb-ass, sorry excuse for birth control, but then he'd never found himself suspended in a semi-imaginary world with a woman who could only be spun from his fantasies.

"I trust your way will be—" her breath hitched when he dipped one finger inside her "—delicious."

Hefting her off the ground, he backed against the wall of rocks behind the cascade of water, hoping she could find a toehold there as he lifted her higher still. Gripping her thighs, he positioned her above his erection—halfway to his freaking neck he was so hot for her—and then lowered her by slow degrees.

He bit the inside of his cheek to keep himself from moving too fast. This couldn't be the way the old-time knights deflowered their maidens. He was moving things along with typical MTV-generation speed, taking her in a pond in the woods when he should have had her wrapped up in a soft bed, or laid out on a bearskin rug in front of a fireplace.

She wound her arms around his neck, fingers clutching at his hair, his shoulders, his back. He could only see her in shadow, but he could still discern the wonder in her expression, her lips parted and her eyes widening a little more with each inch.

She flinched as he hit the barrier. Or maybe it was he who flinched, because the abrupt halt in his entry startled him even though, logically, he should have been expecting it.

"Sorry." He held her steady, waiting for her to be okay with this, waiting for the coronary that was sure to come if he held back much longer.

"I'm not. I'd only be regretful if you stopped." She speared her fingers through his hair and leaned in to kiss him, her wet skin sliding along his while she nipped at his lower lip.

And then, right before his heart was about to launch

clear out of his chest, he thrust forward at the same time he brought her down the rest of the way. The slight resistance he felt before the barrier tore away heaped guilt on his shoulders, but damnation, he couldn't quit now when she pulsed all around him with sensual tremors.

He'd staved off the need as long as he could and now the fierceness of it rolled over him with full force. He gripped her hips with both hands, guiding her where he wanted her. Needed her.

Her body clenched his so tightly, so sweetly, that every thrust wrought a new depth of satisfaction and a powerful hunger for more. His desire for her was deep, primal, assuring him on every level that he'd been transported through time. How else could he account for this primitive need to take and possess, conquer and keep?

Her nails sank into his shoulders, as if she felt the same savage instinct, and her cries became more frenzied. He gave her more, harder, faster and nearly lost control at the same time she cried out with her own release. He couldn't have contained the hoarse shout that rose in his throat as he pulled out from her if he tried, their voices raised to howl at the moon in a whole new way.

The moment blinded him with its raw intensity as he finished, holding her up above him to keep her as protected as the moment allowed. The force of his release staggered him as he held her tight, his face so close to breast level, he couldn't resist taking a taste while his heart slowed down.

Their breathing matched each other in raggedness and he remained there in the water for long moments before he put her on her feet.

"You left me at the last." Linnet's voice loomed soft and vaguely accusing in the darkness. Moonlight lit her pale hair to a ghostly shade as she bent to douse a last splash of water on herself.

Another surreal moment. The black-and-white tones half suggested he'd fallen into a dream.

"I was trying to protect you." He rinsed off as well, the water seeming colder now that the fire of red-hot lust had been sated for at least a little while.

"I wanted you to show me everything and yet you spent your seed in the water in a way that robs me of a true mating."

Ah, damn. He'd hurt her and hadn't even realized it. He should have known a medieval maiden would think differently about sex.

"I promised to keep you safe." He slid a comforting hand over her shoulder, not sure how to make her understand without indicting himself as a man who wouldn't be sticking around. Modern women expected that. But more and more, he realized Linnet didn't think like them. "I didn't want to compromise you that way when your life holds so much uncertainty right now. You're not even sure where you're going to live."

The words sounded like what they were—lame excuses for the core issue that he wouldn't be staying in her world for long.

"Do not mistake me." She walked out of the water

like a nymph, her body glistening with moisture and pale nakedness. "What we shared was the most beautiful experience of my life."

At least that was more like it.

"But?"

"When something is so profound, you rather wish to see how it turns out in the end." She slid into her clothes and left her laces untied while he tromped up the bank feeling decidedly put-out.

Her words shut him up in a hurry. How could he write off her response as a simple lack of sex education when he too had wanted to stay inside her with a fierceness he'd never felt in his life?

When he said nothing, she cleared her throat softly.

"I have offended you."

"Hell no." He kissed her gently as he picked up his sword. "You gave me the most incredible gift any woman could give a man."

He hadn't said it to be Joe Romance, but damned if he didn't think it was true. Besides, hanging out with a twelfth-century female could make a man see the world a little differently.

Maybe he'd be throwing around *thee* and *thou* before all was said and done, too. At the very least, he knew he wouldn't be the same man on the inside once he made it back to L.A.

"I fear I gave you a few scratches as well." She took his hand as he led her toward her brother's house for the night. "The passion between a man and woman is more wild than even my dreams showed me."

"It's not like that with just any man and woman." He paused now and again as they trekked through the woods, listening for any sign of company that didn't walk on four legs.

"Is that so?"

"Sure it is. Being a virgin, you wouldn't know that. But what we shared—that doesn't happen with everyone." Witness his whole sex life up until now. Then again, maybe people lived harder in the Middle Ages because they didn't live as long. That could make sex all the more phenomenal when every encounter took on a live-for-the-moment quality.

And while the notion made him want to take Linnet back to Hollywood with him to guard her and make sure she lived to be a hundred and ten, at the same time, Graham acknowledged there had to be something more substantial beneath their kind of chemistry than just an increased passion for life.

He'd be seeing stars for another week after that encounter. Or, maybe the sex had seemed so good simply because it was fantasy sex and Linnet Welborne wasn't any more real than his wild imagination telling him he was walking through old-time England with a sadistic knight on his trail ready to go medieval on Graham's ass—quite literally.

"So you think our consummation was exceptional." She sounded pleased by this as she hastened her step now that they'd reached the edge of the forest and walked along the fringe of the path they'd taken to the creek earlier in the day.

"I know it was exceptional. And so will you next time you meet a guy who doesn't come close to lighting your fire like me." He tried to keep the observation light even though the words stuck in his throat.

Pissed him off.

"I will do no such thing. I don't plan to ever let any man touch me but you."

Shock and pleasure at his words warred with automatic denial and abject fear that she'd let the encounter mean too much when he really had to find his way home. Sooner rather than later.

"What do you mean?" He nearly tripped over a tree root, he was so surprised by her declaration. "You know I can't stick around since I have to return—"

She brushed her fingers lightly over his shoulder to encourage his gaze.

"My homeland is different from yours, Graham. I will not be able to give myself to another man so simply as I could with you. Any English knight who claimed me would try to barter me from my brothers or otherwise own me and I cannot ever risk that." Her slippers fell silently on the wet grass as she walked slowly beside him.

He waited for her to continue, not having a clue what to say.

"After you leave—" she ducked beneath a low branch "—I will need to keep my identity secret and if I cannot find work in London, I may have to join an order of holy women. As you say in your land, 'trust me,' there will be no opportunity for sex in the convent."

She didn't wish to trap him into marriage or keep him in her crazy fantasy-dream world at all. She just planned to give up sex for all eternity following her encounter with him.

"So in other words, you want a few good memories to perk up your nights in the nunnery?" He shook his head to clear it of the cobwebs, wondering if she was for real. Who went from a chastity belt into a convent after discovering the kind of mind-blowing sex they'd just shared?

Hell, he would gladly give his right arm for a few more nights of bliss with her and she was ready to write it all off as some kind of filler activity before she swore off sex forever?

He didn't know whether to be really insulted that she'd suggest such a thing, or if he should beat his chest with the knowledge no other man would ever touch her the way he had. Damn selfish of him, yes, but he couldn't deny the sense of possessiveness she inspired.

"I suppose you could say that." She hooked her arm through his to walk closer to him, bringing her breasts within touching range of his arm. "But mostly I just shared that bit of knowledge with you so that you could be forewarned I will desire every bit of sexual fulfillment I can garner before I must take a job or holy orders."

Nonstop monkey sex with the hottest woman he'd ever met?

He'd have to be the village idiot to say no. Linnet Welborne was the personification of sexy. And he didn't have a shot at walking away from her without fulfilling that particular request. Just as long as he kept in mind that he couldn't remain here for long, not when his investigation demanded his return. He'd just follow this surreal experience until he found the answers he needed for his case.

And if that involved a lot of hot sex along the way— well hell. That was just a rare and lucky break.

9

SHE WOULD HAVE PREFERRED a broken leg to a broken heart, but Linnet realized she might be doomed to suffer both as she scaled the narrow log up to the second-story balcony of the dark, fortified holding.

Graham steadied her from behind whenever she lost her footing on the precarious crossing, but each brush of his hands on her hips only made her more uneasy inside, the light caresses a bittersweet reminder of all they'd shared. As she righted her feet on the plank a third time, she told herself not to think about the way Graham had withheld himself from her at the last during their unforgettable encounter in the water.

"Are you all right?" He spoke softly in her ear now, a dark shadow over her shoulder as she edged forward more carefully. His voice sent a pleasant shiver through her despite the warm night air.

"Fine." An outright lie, but there seemed no good way to list all the reasons she was *not* fine when their safety might depend on their ability to remain quiet.

Because although Graham had looked around the house before he'd allowed her to approach it, there remained a small chance Kendrick and his men could be out there. Searching for her. For *them*. And the thought of anything happening to Graham began to seem more untenable than any injury Kendrick could possibly do to her.

"Almost there." His words of encouragement rang hollowly in her ears as her fingers searched for grip on the stone parapet. Loose rocks crumbled away before she found a secure section and leaped onto the same low balcony where they'd entered the house for the first time.

Graham dropped down beside her with a soft thud, his grace and balance surprising for a man of his size since he wasn't much shorter than her brothers, all of whom were acknowledged beasts by most people's standards.

They worked silently side by side to make preparations for sleeping. They had stuffed his shirt with tall grasses on their trek back from the pond so they had something soft to make a bed.

Together.

The idea filled her with trepidation for her heart since she couldn't afford to care for a secretive foreigner who would only leave her. Yet she couldn't deny the leap of her pulse as she thought about sharing a blanket with him.

Turning on her heel, she sought her traveling bag with clean clothes, a comb and some mint leaves when a flame sparked within the chamber behind her.

Fire?

Graham seemed to have found a way to light an old taper that rested cockeyed against one wall and she hadn't even heard him strike a flint. Curious.

Even more curious was his effect on her—the same one he'd had from the first time she'd seen him in her wardrobe. Her senses heightened the same way they did in a meadow before a thunderstorm. The air became charged and heavy, making her skin hum with anticipation.

"Do you need any help?" The low timbre of his voice stoked the fire inside that had been banked since the encounter in the waterfall.

"No." She told herself to look away from him, to break the heated spell. "I'm just—"

"Tired?" He moved toward her bag and passed it to her. "We've been awake for so long it's a wonder we're even making sense anymore."

"My thoughts have been so full of other things—" like *him* "—that I hardly had time to think about sleeping. But now that you mention it, I am tired."

She should sleep—prayed for sleep—so she wouldn't have to think about a future that confused her. Scared her.

Where would she go? She hadn't even considered a holy place until the words had passed from her mouth today, but she had reached for any vision of the future that would be safe, one where Kendrick couldn't reach her.

Reason told her she could never be accepted into any prestigious nunnery without a dowry to offer the church, but perhaps if she offered to work hard she could take on a small role?

Blast.

She could not even convince herself. How would she convince any holy woman worthy of her wimple that she would be a dedicated nun? More than anything, she wanted to wrap herself around Graham and find the magic he'd shared with her earlier....

Now, she combed her hair and shared her store of mint leaves with him as a wave of undeniable exhaustion overtook her. She hadn't realized she'd fallen asleep untangling her tresses until Graham pried the comb from her listless fingers.

Too tired to turn away his help, she allowed him to remove her surcoat and kirtle, leaving her garbed in a thin shift of the softest lawn. Even half-asleep, she felt her breasts tighten at the barest brush of his efficient hands.

When he lifted her in his arms, she snuggled shamelessly against him, delighted to find him quite naked against her as he carried her back to the bed they would share for the night.

The scent of fresh cut grasses and clean male skin brought a contented smile to her face as she burrowed closer to him. His soft groan pleased her and, despite a niggling fear that he would soon leave her with naught but a broken heart, she promised herself that tomorrow morning she would use her every feminine wile to make the man remember her for the rest of his natural life.

GRAHAM'S THOUGHTS WERE STILL back in Linnet's bed the next morning as he prowled the grounds around the stone house just past sunrise.

Exhaustion had claimed him for a few hours the night before, but he'd awakened before dawn with Linnet spooned against him, her rump curved into his lap to graze a raging hard-on. His arm had found its way around her during the night, his hand palming her breast. And while he'd far rather be inside her right now than foraging for food or devising a way to use a ground-level door to the house without leaving signs of entry, he figured she deserved her sleep after they'd been awake for so long. Besides that, last night had been her first time—a fact that still blew his mind.

Now, he left a rabbit outside the back entrance to the house and wished like hell he could have just gone to Waffle House for breakfast instead. His mother—so protective of everything and everyone but herself—would have been appalled to know he'd taken down Thumper. But what else could he do? There were no Cheerios in Linnet's world that he could see. No Starbucks drivethrough window with a coffee-and-bagel special.

If she was a reenactor, she was getting a hell of a lot of backup to deliver a convincing setting to go along with her act. But last night as he'd stared at her while she'd slept, he'd turned over and over the idea that she was faking the medieval-maiden persona and he couldn't make himself buy it. What motive could she—could anyone?—possibly have to pull such an elaborate ruse?

Weary of searching for plausible ideas, he released the enigma of his whereabouts for now and focused on the breakfast he'd had to hunt down.

He'd made the switch from carrying his sword in a protective case on his back to wearing it strapped on his waist. As an avid weapons collector, Graham owned plenty of carry pouches for his guns, knives and even swords. But the sheathes you could wear at your side for the swords had always been strictly novelty until now—fun movie props for guys like Brendan.

Graham had to admit he appreciated the easy access to his weapon in an uncertain place. The blade grazed his thigh with each step now, and as he trudged from the house back toward the path to the creek, it occurred to him that being here was a hell of a lot like living in the Middle Ages. He pressed his thumb to the bridge of his nose to ward off an idea that didn't make sense.

Did that mean he was in denial? Or simply losing his mind? As long as he solved his case and found out whatever he could about the connection between what was happening here and what was happening in L.A., he didn't care. He searched the dew-covered grasses along the path leading to the water, thinking maybe he could find some trace of the riders who'd torn through the woods the day before and scared Linnet so badly she'd trembled until her teeth had threatened to shake loose from her jaw.

Tamping down his anger, he sifted through one patch of grass after another for any clues, coming up dry until the ground vibrated against his feet with rhythmic pounding.

Hooves trotting.

Ducking back into the cover of trees, he waited to see the rider. Could it be Kendrick? One of Linnet's brothers?

But this man was neither. A lone stranger on horseback, the rider bore no standard like the pompous, flag-carrying crowd who'd raced past the creek yesterday.

And since no one else knew to connect Graham to Linnet, he made a quick decision to approach the newcomer. Stepping from the trees, he was glad he'd converted his sword to his waist; the same way the longhaired stranger wore his weapon. The blade the other dude carried was customary for a nobleman, with jewels at the hilt and gold inlaid along the handle.

A piece Graham would have given his right arm to purchase at a trade show since goods like that were so rare they stayed in museums or private collections unless an owner died.

"Excuse me." Graham shouted to the young knight who was probably around twenty-five and carried himself like a rookie—all attitude and only negligible skills to back it up. It was obvious by the way the guy started that he hadn't expected company.

Spinning his horse to face Graham, the man's expression turned from vague unease to smug overconfidence. The number-one cause of rookie injury and/or death. Graham was willing to bet it was as true for newbie knights as it was for cops-in-training.

"I am in a hurry to attend an important lord's Midsummer festivities this day," the knight returned from the lofty height atop his massive warhorse's back. "What say you?"

"I'm afraid I took a spill and find I'm disoriented." Graham rubbed his head for dramatic effect, figuring he had to possess at least as much acting talent as brainless Brendan even on his worst days. "Could you tell me what day it might be?"

"Tonight is Midsummer's Eve, sir. Has your fall rendered you deaf as well?" The rider shook his head impatiently and turned his mount back toward the path.

"How about the year then?" Graham had already come to believe Linnet's assessment, but perhaps he asked out of morbid curiosity. A pessimistic need to remind himself his life was seriously messed up right now.

"It is the year of the Lion-Heart's reign, 1190." The guy held his horse back just long enough to give Graham's threads a once-over with a sniff. "And tell your lord to join us. Lord Kendrick has returned from Crusade and is rumored to host a gathering unlike any other. A veritable garden of earthly delights if the tales can be trusted."

The stranger took off so fast he apparently didn't hear Graham's shouted request to wait. He needed more information. Like where the hell this shindig was taking place. The stranger rode in the opposite direction from where Graham and Linnet had seen Burke Kendrick riding the night before.

Cursing his lack of a horse—or a Jeep, damn it— Graham hastened his step back to where Linnet rested. He'd discover some logical way to get himself out of 1190 soon. But for now, he planned to take this opportunity to find Kendrick for himself because, somehow or another, Linnet's former fiancé held a key to Graham's case.

And since Graham had traveled back in time nearly

nine hundred years to find it, he figured this had to be a hell of a clue. He just prayed he'd find a way to get back to L.A. so that once he uncovered the secret origins of the Guardians, he'd be able use the information to bust them permanently.

Too bad the thought of leaving Linnet to do his job already twisted his gut.

"YOU'RE NOT LEAVING WITHOUT ME." Linnet warded off the bout of panic sliding up her throat at Graham's suggestion he follow some flap-mouthed traveling reveler to pursue her former betrothed.

He had descended on her small cookfire like a ravenous beast, promptly devouring his share of the rabbit he'd left near the back entrance earlier that morning. Now, she picked at her breakfast with little appetite, her worries outweighing her hunger as they conversed in the overrun kitchen gardens just outside the holding's stalwart walls.

"You'll be safer here if Kendrick's there." Graham stomped out the last remains of the blaze now that he'd finished his food, his eyes shifting toward the horizon. "Besides, I only have one horse."

"You commandeered a horse?" She regretted sleeping late since she'd apparently missed all the good adventures. She had been looking forward to waking up in bed with Graham, and had found herself deserted with only a dead rabbit for company.

The day was off to an ominous start.

"I didn't find it, exactly. She discovered me when her

rider thought he could separate me from my sword." He grinned and patted the hilt of the weapon in question. "Bad decision for that dude. But it turned into a nice little windfall for us. With no lock-up handy for punishment, I figured a little frontier justice would do the trick."

"Dude? Frontier?" She did her best to understand him, but his words confused her.

"Sorry. That's a tricky one to explain. It means old-school justice. Like the kind your ancestors would have doled out."

She nodded, understanding the concept well enough but frustrated she did not know where words like *frontier* originated. He did not sound like any foreigner she'd ever met.

"Thieves and bandits deserve to be punished. But where's the horse?"

"I left her tied to a tree on the far side of the house so she wouldn't attract attention if riders pass by." He passed her a bucket of water he'd hauled from the creek. "There's a lot of traffic hauling through here on the way to the Midsummer shindig."

"But you cannot follow the trail without me." She had been guarded for so long—in the cruelest ways—that the thought of being completely alone now made her uneasy.

Was that so wrong? She wanted independence. Just not quite yet. And never while Graham encountered danger by himself.

"I'll come back after I scope out the party and I can

take you wherever you want to go. Anywhere you think will be safer than here."

She shook her head, a bad feel insinuating itself in her veins as she idly pried an intrusive thorny vine away from an old sweet pea patch.

"My brothers could find me while you are gone." She'd deliberated long and hard about whether or not to risk making a fire when her kin could be looking for her, but hunger had won out over any need to hide their presence.

"You don't think they will be with Kendrick?" He stilled his restless roam around the clearing behind the house, his whole body tense.

"I am certain Kendrick won't let them back in his presence until they deliver me as promised." Her clan would lose gold, influence and prestige if they couldn't provide one of the most powerful lords in England with his bride.

"Shit." He searched the landscape with his eyes and then tucked her under his arm to plant a kiss on her head. "They're not going to find you."

She warmed at his promise even as she felt guilty for drawing him into her problems.

"I swear I will not remain a burden to you for much longer, but thank you for your protection until I can establish myself in a new life."

He was quiet for so long she angled away from his arm to peer up at him.

"Will you take me with you?" She hoped that was his decision because she feared the worse for Kendrick's Midsummer celebration. She could stand on the fringes of whatever debauchery he had planned and thank the saints she had escaped it.

"Damn straight you're going with me." His hand spanned her waist as he held her in front of him. "But you stick to my side the whole time."

Heat blossomed inside her in spite of any fears about her future. The man had a gift for arousing her.

"I should think that will be a pleasure." She would much prefer dragging Graham back into the house and disrobing him to see if he was as magnificent as she remembered.

Perhaps her wishful thought showed in her eyes for he pulled her against him and lowered his mouth to hers. The soft pressure of his lips brought to mind his consummate skill in pleasuring her. He seemed to know precisely when to deepen the kiss, taking possession of her mouth with the same expertise he'd used to possess her body.

The scent of smoke and fire clung to his clothes. Or perhaps she merely incinerated at his touch. Need rose quickly at just a simple kiss, as if now she knew what other delights awaited her, she couldn't wait another moment to experience them.

He tasted of the sweet wine they'd shared, the grapes heady and intoxicating as his tongue played in a leisurely dance that left her breathless. His corded muscles tightened under her fingertips, the ripple of strength tantalizing her.

Perhaps she felt as good to him as he did to her, for

his hands caressed her with light touches that set her senses on fire. Sweeping up her back and across her shoulders, stroking the column of her neck, his touch moved hungrily over her body until he worked his way down into the neckline of her kirtle.

A whimper issued from her throat, frustration at the layers of clothes between them, making her impatient. But hers were not the garments of a lowborn maid that could be easily pulled down for immediate access. There were laces and ties and brooches to hold it all together.

He palmed her breast through the fabric of her kirtle, her surcoat falling away just a little thanks to Graham's familiarity with her gowns. Heat speared through her more urgently now and she arched up closer to him to convey her desperate situation.

He lifted his head to look down at her, his gaze heavy-lidded and fierce. She could have fallen right inside that gaze, her heart galloping heavily in her breast as she awaited more of his touch.

Just then, a flock of birds startled out of the nearby meadow, their flapping wings beating in rapid time with her pulse as she stepped nearer to Graham.

He reached for his sword as the birds flew off in a cloud of gray and brown. If they were beset by thieves—or worse—Graham would be prepared.

He stayed there, as still as a statue, for a long moment. Listening and watching, he inspected their surroundings before slinging an arm around Linnet again.

"Sorry about that." He shook his head as if disappointed with himself. "We could have been surrounded and I would have never known because all I could think about was tasting you."

His gaze fell to her lips, her breasts, and then whipped back up to her face.

"I am only sorry we couldn't continue." She knew he would not drag her off into the house the way she wanted. Not when he pursued Kendrick or whoever else was behind the crimes in his homeland.

He stepped away from her, the regret in his eyes soothing her disappointment just a little.

"Our time will come." He righted her gown that had slid off one shoulder. "You can count on it."

She didn't know how she'd wait. Especially if she'd be sharing a horse with him all day on the ride to Kendrick's holding.

She began to follow him away from the clearing when he stopped. Pivoted on his heel to face her again.

"And about the nunnery?" He shook his head. "Not gonna happen."

Remaining silent, she didn't bother arguing since she guessed he would not stay with her long enough to enforce his wishes. Instead, she turned into the house to retrieve supplies for the trip, her body still tingling from his kiss despite the memory of a vision that had come to her that morning as she'd gazed into the flames of her cookfire. The Sight told her that no matter how much Graham wanted her now—or how much he protested her convent escape to elude Kendrick forever—

the day would come when Graham would leave her world as quickly and as abruptly as he'd arrived in it.

And she planned to protect herself at all costs so that he did not leave with her heart as well.

10

IT WAS AN IMMUTABLE LAW of universal truth. Riding thirty-some miles with the object of your fantasies perched on your lap would have been torture in any century.

Graham gritted his teeth to maintain control while Linnet's breasts jiggled against his chest, her rump slapping rhythmically against his thighs in an erotic pantomime of sex as they cantered through an open field. They'd started out their journey with her riding behind him, but the sweet agony of her breasts against his back had had him sweating within five miles. Then his brain had fixated on the knowledge of her widespread legs behind him and he'd nearly run the horse under a branch low enough to take off their heads.

Lesson learned. He'd figured he might do better with Linnet in his lap.

Yeah, right.

"Other riders approach," she whispered in his ear, burrowing even closer in an effort to keep her face hidden.

With no trees nearby, they would have no choice but to brazen out any chance encounter. They'd witnessed nearly twenty riders heading toward Kendrick lands throughout the day, but always before, they'd been able to take cover to avoid the possibility of anyone asking their business or recognizing Linnet.

"We'll say you're sick. Just cover up and stay close to me."

The sound of hooves and laughter approached as the riding party drew near. Graham kept his focus ahead, ignoring the noise until raised voices shouted close behind.

"What's this? Another Midsummer reveler bringing a choice morsel to the feast?"

The voice was that of a young man, but Graham didn't turn to look at him until the rider reached his side.

A thin-faced knight with a bloodred shield reminiscent of Kendrick's standard appeared. The newcomer's device depicted a rose and a sword Graham noted as the man drew his mount close, his attention focused solely on Linnet. Graham might have dealt with him more charitably if the heavy-metal wannabe hadn't decided to reach out a hand to place on Linnet's leg.

"I'll only take one finger the first time you touch her, son." Graham hadn't worked on the police force for a decade without learning a thing or two about scaring the pants off testosterone-burning dumb-asses. "But I guarantee the second time you try it, you can kiss your whole hand goodbye."

Heavy Metal pulled back his hand just in time to save his digit while his friends hooted with laughter behind him. Graham still didn't look back, but he would guess there were four or five others. Two of them had to be loaded down, their horses' steps heavier and slower.

"You won't be so possessive` tonight, when the women are brought forward to share." The guy gripped his sword, his knuckles ripped and raw as if he'd used them recently. "Lord Kendrick is reputed to deal harshly with any man too selfish to bring an offering for all."

Linnet flinched in Graham's arms at the name. Or maybe it had been the image of women being passed around for all to share.

But he could offer little comfort now when he needed all his attention on warning away the vipers circling them.

"Selfish?" Graham cracked a smile with calculated superiority. "Hell, boy, don't you know Kendrick himself locks up his favorite so that no other may touch her? Privileges are always granted to any man strong enough to fight for what's his."

He tipped his head in friendly warning before slowing down his mount abruptly to let the others pass. Fortunately, they did so without turning back to lift their swords and avenge the insult Graham had delivered as politely as the situation warranted.

Another crisis averted.

Except that, as he watched the horses trot past, he realized that two of the riders in the group also carried women across their laps. Just like Graham.

Only these women didn't look to be simply hiding their faces like Linnet. They appeared to be drugged or knocked out, their bodies limp and unmoving as they were jostled by the horses' gait over uneven terrain.

"They share the women?" Anger simmered through him as they rode, the heat of his fury blasting away his need for Linnet the way nothing else could have. "What the hell kind of twisted bastard were you going to marry?"

She stirred in his arms now that the other riders had disappeared from sight.

"I don't know, but if I remember correctly, the Kendrick lands should start shortly. There is a small creek that marks the southern border." She squinted into the distance, shading her eyes from the setting sun.

The creek came into view some few moments later. The scent of balefires drifted on the breeze as they closed the distance between them and whatever screwed-up skin parade passed for a party in Kendrick's book.

Graham dropped a kiss on Linnet's head and gave her the squeeze he couldn't earlier. She deserved so much better from life than this. As much as he liked her peculiar turn of phrase and her sexy medieval clothes, he wanted to see her safe and sound in the twenty-first century where men could not take such advantage of women.

And now he had to admit that his reasons for journeying to this place on the other side of a painting hadn't been all selfish. He would do more than solve the case of the Guardians tonight. He was going to keep Linnet away from the scumbag bastard who'd wanted to hurt her, and he'd gladly set free as many other innocent women as he could in the process.

Whether or not he was in his jurisdiction, "protect and serve" still applied.

SHE'D BEEN BETROTHED to a monster.

Linnet had known it in a peripheral way all along, but as she stood on the fringes of his lewd display of carnality thinly disguised as Midsummer festivities later that night, she comprehended the depths of Burke Kendrick's dark soul all the more completely.

"Let me get you out of here." Graham whispered in her ear from behind, her body pressed between his tall breadth of sinew and a fat oak tree off to one side of the gathering. A cool breeze broke the warmth of the night while they watched the "revelry."

Acrid smoke hung in the air from too many balefires, the scent burning her eyes while the thick clouds of gray billowed through the clearing like the wrath of God at the current sacrilege. The pagan trappings of the ceremony were not an issue since the Church turned a blind eye to many a favored old ritual practiced in the rural parts of the land.

No, the sacrilege here came in the form of twisting a beloved ritual into something unholy, since the traditional Midsummer songs and blessings had been eschewed for a parade of feminine flesh before a gathering of unscrupulous men. At the center of the dancing women—who ranged from completely naked to covered by carefully positioned scraps of cloth—Linnet's former captor reigned supreme. Clad in somber colors and a cape adorned with the same intricate symbol Graham had noted on her hated Initiator, Kendrick stood in the middle of the women who writhed and danced through the smoke as if drunken and dispossessed of their wits.

"Nay. I cannot leave." She tipped back to answer Graham as softly as possible, mindful of the revelers who conducted their rituals some forty feet away. "If even one of these women has suffered to take my place here tonight, I cannot simply walk away to leave her helpless to the fate."

After knowing that kind of helplessness herself, she found herself indignant—nay, furious—at the thought of another woman subjected to such bone-chilling fear by the monster parading as a man called Kendrick.

"You're sure as hell not getting involved in this." Graham's grip on her was ironclad, delivering his message more insistently than his words. "And I'm not going to be able to help her either if I think for a second that you're contemplating moving out of this spot."

Unable to answer, Linnet simply stared in stunned silence as the spectacle increased in frenzy, the soft chants from the male onlookers growing louder, their hands reaching out to touch the women whereas before they had merely watched. The dancing females seemed to lose their worries and the remainder of their linen coverings at the shouted encouragement from the crowd, their movements turning more sexual as they cupped their own breasts for better display.

Or, perhaps, for pleasure?

"Do you think they are not unwilling?" Confused by the wanton display of overt sexuality when some of the same women had to be dragged out into the center of the clearing at the beginning of the evening, Linnet hugged her arms tighter around herself. The scene disturbed her and she feared they had not yet seen the worst of it.

"They're drugged." Graham sounded sure of himself as he squinted into the smoke.

"With an herb? With too much wine? How do you know?" She had once imbibed too liberally at a holy day feast and the spinning head she'd received in return had not inspired her to rip her clothes off and caress herself in front of an eager crowd of men.

"I've seen drugs act like this in my country. You can tell by the eyes. The wild movements of their bodies." He stroked her hair as he spoke, offering silent comfort.

"What's he doing?" Linnet saw Kendrick disappear into a brightly decorated tent off to one side of the circle but still in clear view of the crowd. Tension crept through her as she dreaded the answer to her question.

Graham said nothing as they watched another man— dressed similarly to Kendrick—lead one woman into the yellow tent as well.

Fear settled in her belly at the thought of what might take place within the walls where the others could not see. Apparently, Graham shared her thought as he tensed behind her.

"Stay here." Graham stepped back from her, eyes on the clearing and the yellow tent where the woman had disappeared with Kendrick. "I can help her, but only if you stay right there and don't move. Don't let anyone see you."

Before she could ask what he was doing, he kissed her hard on the mouth and then sprinted off into the night, dodging view by running from tree to tree around the perimeter of the clearing.

She cursed him for an errant lout even as she prayed for his safe return. Someone needed to help that woman. All the women. Some men Linnet recognized to be Kendrick's closest knights circulated among the crowd to discourage the most aggressive of the men from pulling the dancing maids into their midst, but the group shouted and strained toward the display so greatly that it couldn't be long before they defied the knights and took turns with the women at will.

Desperate for a glimpse of Graham, Linnet finally caught sight of him on the move again, slipping away from the ring of swords and shields the attendants had been forced to make with their weapons before they were allowed into the festivities. A small fire now burning behind Graham illuminated his movements. Unsure what he thought to do with the little blaze set among the swords and shields when so many others were already lit around the clearing, she watched him tug a keg of ale toward the small fire and then roll it into the middle.

Not until the ale exploded in a shower of flames did she appreciate the beauty of the plan. He'd started a fire right beside the pile of weaponry where Midsummer revelers had been asked to leave their swords. By the ensuing stampede toward the blazing blades, Linnet suspected she and Graham would now have a few moments of time to free the women.

How wrong she was.

As she darted toward the clearing where the dancing women now wandered dazed, aimless and momentarily unguarded, a strong arm yanked her back into the shadows.

"I'd know this fair hair anywhere." The cruel voice chilled her as much as the feel of chain mail biting into her back where a man—a young warrior—held her fast. "'Tis the lofty prize that would not be shared with mere mortals."

She struggled to look into the face of her captor and knew she was seeing the man who'd taunted Graham on the road earlier when she'd hid in his arms.

With no such sanctuary now, she had no wits to rely upon but her own. They might have been enough if his next words hadn't chilled her to the core.

"I think Lord Kendrick will be most grateful to me for bringing him a prize like you."

That she could not allow.

Memories of intimate imprisonment and long days of fear and anguish assailed her. With no time to think, no room for fear, Linnet only comprehended that she could not allow Kendrick to discover her presence. Closing her eyes, she simply rammed her knee upward with all the force she could muster, planting a blow to the knight's manhood as she prayed for release.

GRAHAM HERDED NAKED WOMEN onto the horses he'd stolen from the back of the clearing while Kendrick's guests struggled to save their weaponry. There were probably bedrolls on some of the knights' mounts, but he could hardly take time to dress the blank-eyed females when their lives were in danger. They were definitely drugged; some of the women pawed at him with restless hands as if they'd consumed the mother of all aphrodisiacs.

Or as if they'd ingested the medieval equivalent of ecstasy. He'd arrested enough kids on the popular party drug to know how it played out for most people, and it mirrored exactly what he'd seen tonight. He just couldn't add up how these women of medieval times could have ingested the drug. And holy crap, he *had* to have traveled to an ancient time to have seen as much medieval weaponry as he'd spied today.

The pandemonium he'd created would wane any moment now, the initial shouts of panic already dying as a few men recovered their blades. He would never have been able to help as many of the women as he had if not for the aid of two of the females who seemed to have shaken the influence of the drug better than the others. They had steered their counterparts away from Kendrick's knights toward Graham.

Now he just needed to get Linnet the hell out of here, and he had two horses saved for that express purpose.

"Graham!" A feminine voice shrieked to him from the fringe of the forest.

Linnet.

He heard his name through a cacophony of much louder shouts, his ear as attuned to Linnet as the rest of his body. Turning toward the sound, he half spun into another man's blade.

"You've taken our women!" The guy shouted like the indignant drunk he was, his blade unsteady against Graham's shoulder.

"No luck with the kind you can't drug into submission?" Graham drop-kicked him in the solar plexus, adrenaline pumping through him so hard he needed to hit *something*.

A drunken lecher guilty several times over of sexual misconduct and probably attempted sex with a minor seemed liked a damn fine target for the fury.

Stepping heavily on the fallen guy's chest as he sprinted away, Graham scooped up the extra sword as he moved in the direction where he'd heard Linnet's voice. He was about to shout for her—the confused crowd controlled the fire well enough now that people were beginning to notice the women had disappeared—but then he caught sight of her.

"Graham." She ran toward him in nothing but her under-dress. Less than the under-dress even. A linen scrap of nothing he could see through at ten paces.

Curses exploded from his mouth—all directed at himself—as he recognized he'd never forgive himself for walking away from her for a second. Hot on the heels of that recognition came the realization that a man pursued her.

Not just any man. The heavy-metal-looking rat bastard who had tried to touch her on the road earlier.

Graham seized his sword with a steady hand

despite the rage exploding in his head at the thought of this son of a bitch touching her after all she'd been through with Kendrick.

"Take a horse," he shouted at Linnet as he steamed past her into the darkness, legs pumping with freight-train force to mow down the man who dared put fear in her eyes again. "Ride like hell."

He couldn't afford to turn and see if she followed through as he'd told her, his whole focus narrowed to a lone target. He didn't have time to mess around when Linnet needed him now.

For a moment, he feared the arrogant excuse for a knight would turn and flee, but the guy dredged up enough gumption to draw his sword as he shouted out over the quieting crowd.

"Lord Kendrick!" The words were an icier threat than anything this kid could muster on his own. And since Graham couldn't wait around to draw more attention toward his escape with Linnet, he had to satisfy his bloodlust with a blow to the guy's head using the blunt edge of his sword.

With more than a little relish, Graham cold-cocked Heavy Metal into last year. The scumbag fell to his knees with a quiet thud, his body crumpling unnaturally on the ground.

A cry went up from the clearing as Kendrick's decorative tent collapsed. Possibly resulting from the support beam Graham had filched out of it when he'd ducked inside to rescue the woman and grab a handful of scrolls stashed in a satchel.

From the middle of that clearing, at the center of the destruction and still visible in the light of five roaring balefires, a man garbed all in black stared out over his ruined party. His fury couldn't have been more obvious if he'd rubber stamped it on his forehead.

The desire to take him out rode Graham hard, but today was *not* the day to engage. Not when Kendrick had fifty-some supporters swarming around, just waiting for their swords to cool and their leader to give them orders. Graham, on the other hand, didn't have squat for backup.

And he couldn't spare the time to clean out the bad guys when Linnet galloped through the forest half-naked. Altering his course, he headed back to the horse he'd kept aside for himself before anyone else spotted him. Fifty-to-one odds sucked, even if most of the fifty jerk-offs were drunk.

Smoke and confusion hung in the air as men shouted to one another and tried to make sense of what had happened. Every now and then he'd hear a scream of pain as someone tried to retrieve their weapon, the handles no doubt red-hot from the blaze Graham had set almost on top of the swords.

Sliding into the saddle as quietly as possible, he urged the horse forward, enjoying the feel of riding even more than driving around L.A. in his pickup. If the animal came with surround sound stereo, he'd be living large.

And damn, but that was the least of his problems. He'd be lucky to find Linnet in the dark. He hadn't gone a tenth of a mile when he heard her voice calling from the trees.

The night was a shade of dark you'd never see in L.A. When the moon hid beneath the clouds, there wasn't a hint of light anywhere now that the balefires were out of sight.

"Over here." She emerged from the trees as he slowed, a dark blanket thrown over her like a cape. She lowered the fabric from her head as he drew close, her pale hair catching the scant moon rays and making her look more apparition than woman.

He touched her to be certain.

Pulled her off her horse and into his arms to be even more certain. He'd ask if she was okay in a minute. He needed to feel for himself first.

His sense of reality was all out of whack from running around in the dark lighting fires and freeing naked women. Hell, his concept of reality had been screwed from the moment he'd fallen into a freaking painting.

"Are you all right?" He reached under the shawl of her blanket to skim a hand over her spine. Her skin felt warm and vibrant. Alive. "I never should have left you."

The night air blew cool against his face and he covered her up again, a belated effort to comfort her.

"I'm so glad you did." She smoothed her hand over his cheek grown rough without benefit of a razor. "I couldn't bear the idea of those women suffering in my place and you freed them. I can't tell you how victorious I feel in my heart to know they were spared a night of abuse at the hands of those men."

"No one suffered in your place." How could she think that? "Kendrick would have corralled more women for his sicko games even if he'd found you."

"Still, I—" She shook her head, her hair spilling off his arm with the movement. "I am grateful for what you did."

"But I let that bastard touch you—"

"He didn't touch me." A small smile touched her lips. "He only touched my garments. You may laugh at the many layers I wear, but they kept the man from getting a firm hold on me. Every time he gathered another fistful of clothes, I wriggled out from that layer until I wore nothing but my shift."

"And then?" Although her smile had given him hope she remained unscathed, he still braced himself for the answer.

"And then I delivered a second crotch-bludgeoning blow to the beslubbering boar pig and ran like the wind." Her grin was wholehearted then, so beautiful it damn near took his breath away.

He wanted to kiss her, to drag her off into the woods and possess her completely, but the rumble of hooves in the distance made that impossible.

"Riders." Her eyes went wide.

He tossed her back on her horse with all haste, hoping he'd stolen good mounts.

"They don't know what direction we took." He hoped. "Stay right by me, and whatever you do, don't look back."

Slapping her horse on the flank, he flicked his reins and launched them both headlong into the darkness.

11

LINNET HAD STOOD STILL for so long in the rear entryway of her brother's fortified holding that her feet cramped with the effort.

Graham had suggested they'd left any possible pursuers far behind since they'd never caught sight of anyone after that initial sound of riders drawing near. Thank God for men's penchant for drunkenness or the two of them would surely be dead. But she'd scarcely breathed the whole way home, her ears constantly straining to hear hints of danger behind them. The same way her ears strained now as she fought off a cramp in her hip.

All remained quiet in the surrounding woods. Night had turned into day during their long ride and Graham had told her to hurry inside the small structure when they'd arrived so he might care for the horses. No doubt he wanted to hide them from plain sight.

Now, Linnet stepped deeper into the dwelling, hoping he would return soon from his task. She craved the security of his arms around her, his touch soothing her far more than the knowledge of his sword prowess. How could she have come to rely upon him—to have feelings for him—so soon after they'd met? Could her decision to trust him be sound when she had so few men in her life with whom to compare him?

Stripping out of her shift, she regretted the need to remain indoors for security purposes since a dip in the creek water would have been ideal to wash away the dirt from the journey.

The sound of a horse clopping across the stone path out front caused her to start, her heart leaping to her throat at the thought of someone finding them here.

Racing to the casement, she spied Graham below, his horse towing an ancient cart that creaked and groaned under an old basin.

A washtub, in fact. The wooden bath was full of water that sloshed over the sides with each turn of the cart's wheels.

That she could smile after all she'd seen and all she'd been through the night before was a testament to the effect Graham had on her. He halted in front of the dwelling to stare up at the stone walls, confusion scrawled in the furrowed lines about his face. Shirtless, his body glistened in the late-morning sun. His slick wet hair appeared darker than usual as he mopped off his damp torso with his crumpled shirt.

Her mood lightened at his thoughtful attempt to deliver a bath to her and she found herself stalking out onto the narrow gallery without a stitch of clothes on her body to cover herself. She pulled her long hair forward in a teasing attempt to shield her breasts, but whatever her tresses didn't cover, she would gladly let him see.

The desire to tempt him stirred along with a need all her own. And, perhaps, she appreciated the chance to make beautiful memories with him to rid her mind of the vulgar images they'd witnessed the night before.

"Have you decided to test my skills at giving a bath?" She wished she could somehow stall time and stretch out this day with him, her anticipation for him marred only by the knowledge that what they shared would only last until he departed for his homeland.

"As good as that sounds, my intentions were purely noble. I thought I ought to show *you* how a bath should be given."

The heat blossoming inside her couldn't have been any more potent if she'd been standing right next to him.

"You're going to give *me* lessons?" She twisted a strand of hair between her fingers and pretended to think it over. "You forget you're talking to an expert, sir."

"I'm pretty sure I've got a few tricks in mind that you haven't seen before." He patted his horse on the neck. "So why don't you tell me where I should line up old Buttercup to facilitate the delivery of your bath?"

"Buttercup? Why not Comet or Firedrake? Devil Warrior, perhaps?"

"This sweet animal that was scared of the waterfall? I think not." His eyes narrowed. "Now, are you going to tell me the trick of getting this tub inside or am I going to have to besiege your castle?"

"As long as I am properly ravished either way, I care not." She slid her eyes boldly down his body and back up again. "Although I am rather eager to wash off."

"If you look at me like that again, I just might forget all about the bath and move straight to the ravishing."

Her knees weakened at the thought and she drew her hair around her breasts more thoroughly to hide her body's response. She wanted to linger in this game, to savor each moment with him.

"Tell Buttercup to back up to the great hall doors and you can put the tub in the common area. It will be easier than a pulley to the second floor."

"And what about the need to hide evidence of our presence?" He studied the roofline as if seriously considering the pulley.

"I think we will leave soon enough, don't you?" They hadn't discussed plans to move on since he'd told her he wouldn't take her to a nunnery, but the knowledge hung over them nonetheless. "Perhaps for one more day we can simply bar the door and hope for the best."

His expression remained inscrutable, but then he nodded.

"Since I plan to spend all day fulfilling your every wish, I'll start with that one."

Within minutes, he had the tub in the great hall in front of the empty fireplace. When he left to secure the horse and the cart he must have found in one of the outer buildings, Linnet climbed gratefully into the tub. The cold creek water chilled her, but she appreciated the chance to wash off the stranger's hands on her—even if they'd been on her clothes and not *her* directly.

She'd brought scant niceties with her upon leaving

Welborne Keep, but between her soap and her comb she would address most of the damage from her journey. She only had one surcoat now that the brutish knave had torn hers, but it would have to do for whatever life she made next.

Fear of the future threatened for only a moment before she forced it back into submission. She would not allow anything to spoil this day with Graham that might be her last.

When he returned, he arrived with a fistful of sweet violet flowers, his other arm full of sticks. At first, she thought he meant to deliver a bouquet, but he simply tossed the lavender colored petals into the tub as he passed her on the way to the hearth.

"They smell delicious." She tipped her head back on the rim of a tub that was too small, her knees bent to accommodate the size.

"You didn't wait for me." He flicked a tiny cascade of water onto her knee with his finger. "I hope you remember who's in charge of the bath. You can't plead you're too cold just because you jumped the gun."

"I jump nothing, sir. I just didn't want you to see me at my dirtiest." She flicked a narrow stream of water at him in return, the droplets landing on his bare back and trickling enticingly down into the waist of his unusual braies that fit his buttocks with extremely pleasing results.

He grinned at her as he tossed the sticks in the fireplace, followed by a fat log that had been left off to one side of the hearth for heaven knew how many years. The timber quickly burst into flame.

"Maybe I like my women dirty." He smiled as if he were privy to a joke she would not understand. "But I hope you'll let me see you any other way I want."

The suggestion made her curious in a shivery way, her skin tightening and tingling as she considered the possibilities those words offered.

Through half-lowered eyes, she watched Graham move around the hearth, his back rippling with intriguing sinew as he worked. His bare chest flushed bronze in the heat of the blaze he created with almost no effort. He seemed to have a tool for every occasion and somehow he possessed a device that must help him create a blaze very quickly. She would have to ask him if he possessed another wondrous instrument from Walmart sometime, but right now she was more concerned with the blaze he'd started inside her.

"That ought to take the chill out of the air." Graham rose to his feet and adjusted one last stick with his boot. "It's amazing how these old stone structures hold the dampness."

"'Tis not so old." She flicked another stream of water at him, ready to retrieve his full attention. "My grandfather commissioned the building as a young man."

Graham turned to face her.

"Then I guess it's not so ancient after all. My mistake." He stalked closer, his gaze never leaving her face despite her nakedness. "How can you sit so leisurely in cold water?"

"I am not a woman of endless means, sir. I can hardly afford the luxury of having my every bath heated."

"Would you like it if you could?" He knelt by her side, picking up the soap she'd left near the basin.

"Bathe in only warm water?" She stared at his hand coming down into the water to touch her, to clean her, and she tipped her head back in sweet abandon to the moment as her eyes drifted closed. "What decadent thoughts you have, Graham Lawson."

"You deserve a little decadence in your life."

Just as she wondered why he had not touched her yet, her tub skidded forward toward the hearth.

She yelped in surprise, the water splashing over the rim of the tub as he carefully lined up her toes in front of the blaze he'd set.

"Now you can be a little warmer at least." He stood back to admire his accomplishment, his gaze lingering over her bare legs and sending awareness skittering up her thighs.

"I have a much better idea for staying warm." The water around her brought back memories of their visit to the creek two nights ago and all the ways being slippery could be pleasurable.

As amazing as those memories were, she wanted to stockpile more to comfort her when she was alone once again.

"You think you've got ideas?" He hooked his foot around a trestle bench and dragged it over to the side of the tub. "I have a notion for dispelling all the ugliness we witnessed last night so that you can go to sleep dreaming about nothing but me."

Touched that he would remember the power of her

dreams and would even consider them now, Linnet blinked back the burning sensation behind her eyes.

"I haven't been able to think about anything but you since we left your ex's bonfire party." Graham leaned close to kiss her knee where it stuck up out of the water, his tongue swirling around her wet skin with strokes that left her light-headed.

"You were overcome by the sight of me in my shift?"

The sight of his lips pressed to her flesh made her shiver. He must have felt her stare since he glanced up to meet her gaze while he licked her.

"I was overcome by a bloodthirsty need to hurt any man who dared to put fear in your eyes." He watched her with dark eyes, his hair outlined by the red glow of flames behind him. He looked otherworldly. Beautiful and dangerous.

"You have been a far better protector than my own kin. A more noble champion than the man I would have wed. And while I wish I could remain within the haven of that security a little longer, I have known from the beginning that you would not linger with me for long."

She wanted to alleviate him of the guilt she saw in his eyes. The regret.

He reached to cup her jaw in his palm, his thumb smoothing the soft hollow under her cheekbone.

"You have had visions of me leaving?" His touch remained gentle, soothing, but she sensed a tension in his question.

"Not in specific images, but the knowledge of your departure lurks in my mind, certain as the sunrise."

What she didn't tell him was the way she'd felt upon his leaving. In her mind's eye, she could almost taste the overwhelming sadness, the unreasonable sense that he wasn't just leaving England but that he somehow escaped into a whole different world where she could never reach him again.

"I have no choice but to go back." He reached deeper into the water to wrap his arm about her waist, his fingers kneading a soft show of comfort when the only thing she really needed now was passion. Only the fiery emotions of desire could erase that gnawing sense of impending loss.

"I know."

Her whispered admission faded into a kiss, him moving forward, her arching up to meet him. She offered her lips, her mouth, without hesitation. How quickly she'd emerged from her virginal captivity to revel wantonly in a man's touch.

And no matter that Graham couldn't stay with her. She wouldn't change one thing about the time they'd spent together.

Well, except for one.

"You will stay inside me this time." She whispered the request—nay, demand—between kisses, her breath coming faster as he stroked the wash linen between her breasts. Down to her navel.

Graham thanked God for the condom in his wallet, not sure how he could have accommodated her request otherwise.

And denying her anything was out of the question.

He practically fell in the water to kiss her, her arms drawing him down to where her breasts peeked out of the bath every time she drew a breath.

His hands sought the soft weight of her cleavage, palming the generous mounds. Fingers sliding over her with ease thanks to the water and soapy lather, he wanted to touch every square inch of her, to know her more intimately than he'd ever known any woman.

A foolish wish when she remained unobtainable for him. Living nine hundred years apart was a long-distance gap no relationship could survive, and he had to return to his life in L.A. He'd swiped a handful of scrolls from Kendrick's private tent at the Midsummer festivities that might hold the key to the perverted history of the Guardians, but he hadn't even opened them yet because he wanted—needed—this last window of time with Linnet before he found some place safe to leave her.

For now, he would indulge himself.

He lifted her out of the tub, the soap and the cloth falling back into the bath as water sluiced over her body. Flower petals clung to her skin. He'd laid some blankets by the fire earlier, knowing he wouldn't be able to make it upstairs with her once he got his hands on her.

"Sorry it wasn't much of a bath but I need to have you close." He kissed her neck as he walked them over to the hearth and the makeshift bed he'd transferred from the upstairs bedroom. "Closer."

She tasted like flowers and clean creek water. He laid her down on the blankets so he could look at her in the firelight, her glistening body catching the glow of the blaze in each tiny droplet on her skin.

"To be truthful, I was most looking forward to what came after the bath." She arched up as he kissed his way down her body, her spine stretching to put her breast closer to his mouth.

As if he needed any encouragement to devour her.

Lips locking around the taut crest, he drew on her hard, nipping the pink bud and then licking away the ache before starting all over again. He lingered there, quickly growing addicted to the throaty sounds of pleasure she made as she arched harder, wriggled closer.

Only when she could hardly be still did he allow his fingers to do some walking. He drifted down over her barely-there belly to circle her hip bones and then sift through the curls guarding her sex.

All his.

He couldn't help the selfish thought that he was the only man to have her, the man she'd chosen for her first time. Her second time. No woman had felt that way about him—wanted him that much—before.

When his thumb hit the soft, swollen nub of her sex she cried out. Tensed. Her fingers gripped his forearms, nails biting into his flesh as she held on tight.

He released her breast to admire the damp glow on her skin, the pink peak straining toward him as if to beg another kiss. If only he had the reassurance of more time with her, another day for more kisses, perhaps it would have been easier to move away, to conquer new terrain on her gorgeous body.

But while every touch electrified his senses, sizzling his nerves into high-voltage attention, those same caresses all burned regret into his skin like a brand. The memories would be imprinted forever, but the making of them would be bittersweet.

"I wish I could take you with me." He spoke the words to her navel as he kissed his way down her abs to the *V* of her thighs.

"Where?" She twitched beneath his touch, her restless moans and sighs a sweet music he wouldn't forget.

She didn't understand and he couldn't explain. She might not believe him. Or worse, she might think he lied on purpose to avoid a commitment. And not for the world would he hurt this woman who had already been through so much.

"Everywhere."

He spread her wide to taste her, his thumbs pushing aside the swollen folds to tease the burning center of her. Her cry filled the small hall, the shout echoing in the rafters above along with a misguided bird who chirped accompaniment.

The hearth fire warmed his back, but not nearly as much as she sizzled the rest of him. He reached down to unzip his fly, his jeans too constraining for the want of her.

But he never released the tight bud that made her squirm, though. She squeezed her thighs to his shoulders, whimpering with pleasure and want while he dipped one finger inside her. And another.

She went utterly still for a moment, her every muscle

tense until the first convulsive shudder rocked through her, a raw cry wrenching from her throat as she found her peak.

He pressed harder against her inner walls, hungry to feel every lush tremor as she twisted against him. When every last spasm had quivered through her, she stirred again, fingers raking his shoulders.

"I want you inside me." Her whispered words were soft, but her movements were still urgent as her fingers dove beneath his boxers to stroke him.

Levering himself above her, he kept his weight on his elbow, more than happy to give her what she wanted. Unable to keep his mouth off her, he kissed her as she touched him. She was so incredibly sweet. His pulse quickened with the desire to consume her, to savor her, taste her everywhere. He sampled her lower lip, her neck. Sucking, licking, kissing.

But if he thought to distract himself from her tentative strokes along the underside of his cock, *ah hell*. He didn't have a prayer.

He released her enough to roll to one side, fishing his wallet from his pocket and his condom from within the billfold.

"I have displeased you?" She frowned at his wallet and the foil packet he withdrew. "You are—too busy to make love to me?"

"Not hardly." He didn't have a clue how he was going to explain as he ripped open the package. "I— uh—have a way to make sure sex doesn't make you pregnant, but allows me to stay inside you."

"You have been to a medicine woman?" She touched the thin prophylactic as he rolled it on. "This fabric has been charmed?"

"Well, it works like a charm, let's put it that way." Tossing the package and his pants aside, he devoted his full attention to her now, his hips settling between her legs, wedging her open.

He could already feel the damp heat of her, and he wasn't even touching her yet. She reached up to thread her fingers through his hair, to tug him closer through force of will if not strength.

"Please." She ground down closer to him and he could not string out the moment another second.

Hips thrusting forward, he entered her slowly, the thrill of being inside her causing lights to flash behind his eyes, his whole body hyperalert to her. Each new inch rocked him a little more.

"I cannot even feel this wondrous device." Her fingers gripped his shoulders as she clung to him. "All I feel is—*ooh*."

He withdrew from her slightly and then pushed his way deeper, farther. Restraint was important if he wanted to make this last—and damn but he had to make it last—yet reserve was tough to come by when she tilted her hips upward, taking more and driving him crazy for her.

"It is pretty wondrous." He could listen to her talk all day long. "But the charm will only work once so we need to make the most of this one time."

"Once?" She looked stricken for a moment, her

whole body going still as she gripped the blankets in their hearthside bed. "Then there is something I must ask you for while you can still grant my request."

"Name it." He was ready to take on fifty knights for her just yesterday—he couldn't imagine anything he wouldn't give her at this moment.

"I have heard it is a sin," she warned him, her green eyes full of dire warning and still so freaking beautiful.

"Yeah? I like it already." He captured her mouth once more for a long, slow, thorough taste.

When he released her, her eyes were less wary and more sex-dazed. Just like he wanted.

"Perhaps I could be on top?" She made the request in a breathless rush.

That was her sinful act?

She was priceless.

"I'd like nothing better than to check out the view of you naked on top of me." He rolled to his side and onto his back, taking her with him until she lay over him, her long hair spilling over his arm. "But I don't know how long I can last with this kind of temptation."

She pushed herself up to sit straight on him, the guilty pleasure of their new position evident in her wicked grin.

"You really let me be in charge." The surprise in her voice renewed his anger at Kendrick for treating her like a possession and fired Graham's determination to show her how a relationship between a man and woman could be.

Should be.

"Yes, ma'am. And I encourage you to have your

wicked way with me." He bracketed her hips with his hands, loving the softness of her oh-so-fine booty under his fingertips. "In fact, the wickeder, the better."

"I'll keep that in mind." She bent down to kiss him, her fingers grazing his unshaven cheeks as she steadied his face.

Tenderness for this woman unfurled inside him, scaring him with its intensity. He shoved those thoughts from his mind even if he couldn't quite obliterate them from his heart.

She sat back on her haunches again, her body outlined by the orange glow of the fire in a room that remained otherwise dim without many windows.

"I hardly know where to begin." She swirled her fingers around his chest to track lower on his abs.

His muscles shivered in response, flexing everywhere she touched.

"You let me know if you need lessons in wickedness." He had plenty of ideas on that score.

"I prefer to acquire firsthand experience." She rode up and down on him for a moment before readjusting her legs, knees bent, so that she could prop herself up on her toes.

Unusual.

And un-freaking-believable.

With the extra leverage of her legs beneath her, she could rise higher on his cock, holding herself above him for long moments before inching her way down so slowly his eyes crossed with the pleasure of it. Taking total control, she rocked her hips up and down, her eyes falling closed as she found her rhythm. A rhythm that made him break out in a cold sweat.

"Is that enough experience for you?" He ground out the words between clenched teeth, staving off his finish that threatened every time she lifted herself high to tease the head of him.

"I don't think so." She slid down him again with smooth grace as she wrapped one hand around the base of him and squeezed him gently. "I'm learning so much."

"Are you prepared to be repaid in kind?" He tried to dredge up those tender thoughts he'd had about her again to keep him from thinking about the mind-blowing sex, but all traces of gentleness had vanished when she'd started her acrobatic tricks that were straight out of a double-jointed fantasy.

"What do you mean?" Her eyelashes fluttered open wide as soon as he grazed her clit with his fingers.

"That's what I mean." He stroked her sleek folds where she stretched to accommodate him, then gave her sex a soft pinch that sent her flying back down into his arms.

He rolled her to her back again in no time flat, needing this control if he wanted to last longer.

"Sorry, sweetheart. Your experience will have to wait."

He drove into her the rest of the way with all the fierceness she'd ignited behind his thrust, his need too raw for finesse anymore. Her eyes rolled back when his body met hers and he sensed he wasn't the only one hanging by a thread.

"Come for me, Linnet." He chanted the request in her

ear as he watched her whole body flush pink with desire. "I want to see you go crazy for me again."

He cupped her hip to drive her closer, then slid his hand between them to pluck the damp fullness of her clit.

She gasped at the contact, her whole body going still again and he knew the end was inevitable. She convulsed around him a second later, her hips lifting, thrusting of their own accord.

He couldn't stave off his release with the blatant sexuality of hers urging him on, taking him to that final level. His finish racked through him like a hammer, pounding out his pleasure with undue force and driving him deeper, hotter, wetter. The sensation blasted away any memory of sex with anyone besides her, their moments together too intense to leave room for any memory that didn't have her in it.

He couldn't think. Couldn't move in the aftermath of their time together. It was all he could do to roll to his side and tuck her warm body against his.

And as much as he wanted to let sleep drag him under with her as her breaths evened into a slow cadence, he owed it to his investigation to crack open the scrolls he'd pilfered from Kendrick's tent.

Regret filling up the hollow places inside him, Graham waited another minute to make sure Linnet was asleep, then eased out from under the covers to discover whatever clues he could unearth on the strangest journey of his life.

12

DARKNESS PREVAILED when Linnet awoke. The sun had gone down, leaving only the light of a dying fire in the hall where she still lay between two blankets.

But worse than the physical darkness was the mental one.

"Graham?" Waking up alone brought back ghosts of the old loneliness that had haunted her since she'd been consigned to a chastity belt.

Nay. If she were honest, the darkness had started when her mother had died, leaving her alone to fend for herself among half brothers who did not love her and a father for whom she was naught but a burden.

"I'm here." His voice kept the shadows at bay a little longer, but she'd had a taste of how her future would feel without him.

Rising to sit, Linnet spied him on the trestle bench before the fire, his hands tilting a piece of parchment toward the dying embers in the hearth.

"You wanted to read Kendrick's scrolls." Graham had mentioned them in passing when they'd shared stories of their time apart. After setting the blaze that had distracted the men and brought Kendrick running into the fray, Graham had run into the private ceremonial tent to drag out the woman Kendrick had brought inside it.

He'd taken the parchments then in the hope they would contain clues.

Clues that would only tear them apart.

"Your former fiancé is amassing a fortune in gold and ancient artifacts." Graham's back took on a bronze hue in the burnished glow of the scant flames. He'd clothed himself in his braies for his late-night reading, but he remained shirtless, a condition which she greatly appreciated.

The mere sight of him sent her pulse skipping.

"I care not what he does so long as he remains far from me." She shuddered, wrapping herself in the blanket Graham had used to cover her. Padding over to sit on the bench beside him, she clutched the blanket like a cape.

"You might be interested in his methods." He passed her one of the parchments, the vellum smooth and soft. "What do you make of that?"

Rotating the scroll to orient herself, she saw it contained a picture. A diagram of a desert and three pyramids with a crude palm tree and crescent moon in the background. At the top of the parchment were the only words on the page, reading simply *Visualize This*.

"I don't understand. What does this have to do with Kendrick acquiring wealth?" She had expected accounting lists or inventories of his holdings, not a poorly sketched picture.

"He has an impressive list of acquisitions on another scroll along with a list of wanted items." Graham flashed another scroll under her nose, this one crammed full of words in an unfamiliar language.

"You can decipher these?"

"You can't?" His demeanor had shifted somehow, becoming more distant.

He was no longer her lover. This was the lawman.

"Some words look familiar, and others do not." She struggled with a few lines and picked out whatever she recognized. "Egypt. Kings. Linnet?"

Was that really her name on the long list of inventory?

"It's a form of English I know well. And yes, that's your name as a notation beside his entry about searching the Valley of the Kings in Egypt."

"Like the picture?" She turned back to the crudely drawn desert scene and suddenly understood. "He wants a woman with the Sight to visualize this valley. He hopes to search for treasure by using me to see it for him."

"I think he drugged those other women last night with something to make them hallucinate so that they'd see visions, too. But I don't know why he'd think he could trust their information if people without an extrasensory gift looked at these pictures."

Graham gestured to a pile of other scrolls in his lap, and only then did she realize how ambitious Burke Kendrick's plans had been. He wasn't just trying to steal valuable artifacts from the resting place of Egypt's kings. He wanted to steal from sites all over the world.

"My mother once told me everyone is born with some potential to have the Sight. But most people ignore the gift in favor of what they see with their eyes until at last the natural ability to see with their minds withers and dies."

She hadn't thought about those old conversations with her mother in a long time, a habit abandoned back when the memory brought with it a pain she could not bear. But the ache was no longer there, replaced by a mellow and comforting warmth, as if she'd healed an old friendship.

And she needed that warmth now when Graham remained subtly distant.

"Did you ever have a friendship with Kendrick? Before he became your enemy?"

Her neck prickled with warning and she hated to feel that kind of uncertainty with the man she'd given herself to, whether he recognized the value of her gift or not.

"Never. May I ask why you would suggest such a thing and why you have backed away from me in your heart even if you haven't left the chamber we share?" Her heart pounded in nervous, jerky beats.

"Speaking strictly from a legal perspective, you're implicated in these writings as a partner to Kendrick. He suggests you've already helped him find many treasures."

"Impossible." She shook her head, disappointed that he would give any credence to outright lies. "I'd never met him before he came to claim me as his future bride.

And even then, he spent little time here. He certainly never asked me to visualize anything for him."

Although he had questioned her extensively about her gift. But she'd already told Graham about that.

Shoving away the scrolls, he nodded.

"Sorry. I knew that. I just— Thanks for clarifying." He pulled her onto his lap and kissed her, the cool reserve gone.

"You are a man who does not trust easily."

She hadn't known that about him, perhaps because they'd had so many other obstacles to overcome in the short time they'd known each other. Now all the customary strategies for courtship no longer applied. They had moved beyond polite dinner conversations in front of their families.

They had slept together without understanding one another at all.

"Lack of trust makes me good at my job." He brushed his lips across her forehead, then rained kisses over her eyes. "I'll admit it sucks when it comes to personal relationships."

"Someone hurt you?" She opened her eyes to watch his reaction.

"No. I'm just careful not to be a sucker."

"Where I come from, we have a name for that." She wrapped her arms around his neck. "'Tis called someone hurt you."

"Okay, put it this way." He reached beneath her blanket to mold a hand to her bare hip. "Maybe someone *tried* to hurt me."

She could almost believe him. But he pushed the fib too far, and his eyes told another story.

"I do not need to know your tale if you do not wish to share it." She sensed what she didn't know about Graham Lawson could fill many tomes. "But I have no reason to deceive you."

He made no answer, but continued his exploration beneath her blanket. His hand dipped between her thighs to cup her mound and she knew he wished to end that particular conversation.

He pressed the heel of his hand against her sex; making her achingly aware how much power he had over her. His need became her need in one intimate touch. He could wrest a cry from her with a single lazy swipe of his finger or a deep, wet kiss.

Both of which he gave her now while she melted into his lap, her blanket falling away along with her fears that he did not trust her. She would muddle her way through it tomorrow, when he was long gone. If she was fortunate enough to have him inside her again tonight, she would accept it greedily.

Already her feminine muscles shivered with hunger. She writhed unabashedly in her seat on his thighs, delighting in the hard feel of him. His tongue flicked over her lips in the same kiss that had driven her mad when he'd delivered it between her thighs, and the memory of that moment was so powerful it made her cry out with want.

The heat between them flared up so quickly, so intensely, they did not bother moving to their makeshift bed. He unfastened his braies and shoved them down while she straddled him.

He didn't enter her at first. Allowing her to rub herself against him, heightening her pleasure and her hunger.

Just when she thought she would go mad without him inside her, he reached behind them to dig in the traveling sack she'd brought from Welborne Keep.

He emerged with the Initiator. The horrid device Edana had laughed about, the one used to penetrate a woman.

"I want *you*." Her thighs squeezed close reflexively, but she only managed to hug his hips because of the way she was seated.

"You have no need to fear it," he whispered in her ear, stroking the outer rim with his tongue between words. "Where I come from, women use these to bring themselves pleasure when they are alone."

"But I am not alone." She stroked the engorged head of his staff. "That piece of wood and horn possesses no warmth. No velvety skin over stiff muscle."

He strained toward her and she rewarded him by increasing the pace of her strokes. Learning what he liked had been a seductive pleasure.

"But I can't come inside you. I have no more of the—uh—medicine woman's charm."

She mourned the loss of his magical thin skin that kept her safe. Opening herself to the lifeless tool seemed far less appealing.

"Besides," he continued, already lowering the rod between her thighs, "this way you will conquer another piece of what made you scared of Kendrick. You can take something he taunted you with and make it a harmless, pleasurable toy to be enjoyed."

A toy?

She raised an eyebrow at his description but protested no further. Her body was already a mass of hot, hungry need.

"Do not hurt me, Graham," she pleaded, closing her eyes to feel what he did instead of see the wicked object in his hands.

"Never."

True to his word, he kissed her lips and mirrored the stroke of his tongue with the work of his fingers on her sex. Soon she was so slick and ready for him that he had no trouble nudging the device a short way inside her.

He held it there, allowing her to become used to the feel of it. While it was a poor substitute for Graham, at least he offered her aching, wanting body a substitute.

He lowered his head to her breast and drew on one tight peak. Her thighs clenched in appreciation of the kiss, edging the rod deeper inside her.

Oh.

"That's it." He rotated the carved wood, allowing her to feel the bumps in the surface.

Now that—that part was actually very nice.

"Don't forget who's touching you, Linnet," he growled softly in her ear, his voice a rugged rasp that made her realize how difficult it must be for him to furnish all the pleasure. "I'd give anything to be inside you right now, to take the place of this carving and bury myself deep."

She trembled in answer, knowing she would soon abandon all dignity to scream out loud with rapture at the wicked penetration. The crisis inside her quickly built to an undeniable peak.

"I wish it could be you." She hissed a breath through her teeth as he massaged the sweet spot between her thighs. "But you are right, the pleasure is not so bad with this and—*oooh*."

She flew apart in a million directions, clinging to him as he pushed the intimate weapon deeper, harder.

When she recovered, she would return his generosity with her hand or her mouth. Whatever he wanted, she would gladly give. He'd taught her a trick she would never forget and by God, she would surely never be afraid of the Initiator again.

If anything, she counted herself grateful to have brought it with her as she embarked on a new life. Her heart might be broken, or at the very least empty, but she would have a naughty little secret to remember Graham by, a decadent reminder of all they had shared.

Head reeling from the furious beat of her pulse, Linnet slid off his lap and sank to her knees in front of him. She would never let it be said that she left Graham hurting, and judging by the look of his staff right now, he had to be experiencing some pain.

Applying her tongue to the task, she vowed to replace it with pleasure.

GRAHAM DOVE DEEP into the cold creek water the next morning, his bathing place well downstream from the scenic waterfall where he'd first touched Linnet.

He wasn't normally a sentimental guy, but today he found he didn't want any more reminders of what he'd be leaving behind if—*when,* damn it—he found his way back to L.A.

To the twenty-first century.

Lathering up his face with the harsh bar that Linnet called soap, he applied her dagger to his cheek in a barbaric attempt to shave. Praying for a steady hand so he didn't slit his throat by mistake, Graham acknowledged he didn't have any clue how to replicate the unorthodox journey he'd made to Linnet's world. How could he leave this medieval time and return to his own?

Hurrying to finish his neck, he hastened his pace to make sure Linnet was safe. He'd made her bar the door, but the fortified holding was hardly impenetrable. He needed to be with her to protect her.

They would be gone soon since he'd agreed to escort her to the next village before he departed to seek a way home. To seek another painting to fall into. Or hell, if need be, he'd try painting his own.

Wading out of the water, he stubbed his toe on a metal object near the shore.

"Damn." He hopped on his good foot, his injured toe catching on still more metal and damn near tripping him.

What the hell?

He released his foot to reach down in the water and lift out the offending object.

Linnet's chastity belt.

She'd flung the thing into the current after he'd freed the lock. It must have floated downstream to land here, perfectly positioned to break his neck. He was about to throw the malicious device deeper into woods so it would not prove such a menace, but before he could release it, a small white tag caught his eye.

While much of the belt was made of metal, some thin, worn fabric still lined the inside of the ring where it would have rested on her hips. The little tag remained intact, however, and something about that crisp white fabric made him pause. Take a closer look.

While one side of the tag was white and unmarked, the other contained letters. Words. Three of them, in fact.

Bold block letters spelled out *Made in Taiwan.*

No.

His brain refused to compute.

Medieval women didn't wear garments with tags that said Made in Taiwan. Modern women did.

Stepping on the belt might not have brought Graham down, but discovering that white tag damn well did. He sank to the warm, grassy bank while still buck naked, his mind struggling to come up with a reasonable scenario. There was none.

He couldn't have traveled through time if he was holding something that had been made in Taiwan. No wonder Linnet hadn't wanted to let him take her belt off for her. She'd been adamant about doing it herself. At the time, he'd written it off as modesty or that she'd been sexually traumatized by her former fiancé. But now?

He didn't know what to believe.

With the discovery of one tiny little anachronism, he had to question the whole medieval backdrop he'd walked into, and he needed to ask himself why anyone would go to such lengths to deceive him.

His movements brittle with numbness at the discovery, he set the belt down and shoved his legs into his pants. Linnet had asked him if he'd been hurt in the past, and he'd been able to deny it last night.

Today, however, was a different story. With the discovery of Linnet's perfidy, Graham had no problem admitting that right now he hurt like hell.

13

SHE WAITED FOR GRAHAM'S TAPS on the back entrance they'd agreed to use for security purposes. Every door and window was barred, including the balcony where they'd originally entered the structure.

Graham had been meticulous in his planning. Which was why her nerves fluttered in warning when the expected knock arrived in a barrage of soft thumps on the front door instead of the agreed-upon rhythmic pattern of knocks on the back door.

Had Graham forgotten their agreement? Could he be hurt and bleeding or chased by thieves? He'd been beset by bandits in these woods before.

"Graham?" She hastened over to the front door, whispering the word through the fat oak barrier, not sure if the sound would carry.

"'Tis your brother," a hoarse voice rasped. "Open up."

"Hugo?" Panic shot through her. She thought it might be the youngest of the brothers, but couldn't be sure.

"Aye. You cannot barricade me from my own fortification." He banged louder, the vibration rattling through the wood a tangible reminder of her clan's brutish ways.

"I can and I will." Indignation straightened her spine. "I will not allow you to hurt me anymore."

Before he could reply, a precise series of knocks sounded at the back door.

Thank God.

Ignoring Hugo's oaths and protests, she skirted the washtub in the great hall to let Graham inside. With an effort, she raised the heavy bar and allowed him in.

"My brother is in the front courtyard." She hadn't realized how much his presence scared her until she heard the tremor in her voice. "I do not know if he is alone or if he brought the others. He may have brought Kendrick himself."

His silence startled her out of her panic, forcing her to take stock of him, his hair still dripping on the floor as he laid his soap on the hearth along with…her chastity belt?

"What is it?" Wary of his mood, she noted the dark look in his eyes. Distant. Suspicious.

She didn't need the Sight to know something had angered him. Unsettled whatever scant affection for her he may have felt. She felt the loss of it clear down to her toes, although it resonated most fully in her heart.

"I will take care of your brother." Pushing past her, he stalked to the front door, his movements brusque, tense.

"He demands entrance," she explained, grateful at

least that Graham would set aside his own frustrations to banish her unwanted sibling.

She expected Graham to deliver a warning. A threat. Some form of verbal sword brandishing that would make Hugo think twice about calling Kendrick down on their heads.

But Graham did not speak a word to her brother. To Linnet's utter amazement, he simply hefted the bar to admit her kinsman.

"Are you mad?" She fought the urge to flee, to hide in a distant bedchamber.

But a rational voice in her head assured her that without Graham's help, she would not be able to escape her family or the man she'd been promised to three years ago.

Hugo stumbled into the hall, clothes torn and filthy, his oversize body covered with massive bruises and oozing cuts.

Graham scarcely spared him a glance while Linnet couldn't help a twinge of sympathy. Her brother was obviously in pain. He looked as if he'd been brutally beaten.

And—thankfully—he seemed to be alone since no one else followed him through the door Graham had flung wide.

"As a matter of fact, I am mad." Graham's voice chilled her skin as he stared right through her. "I'm downright pissed off that you would try to pull a stunt like this to waste my time when I have an ongoing investigation where lives are at stake."

"I don't know what you're talking about," she protested, bewildered at this new turn. Where was her lover? Her champion?

"I don't even bloody well understand him." Hugo slumped onto a trestle bench, his movements slow and weakened from blood loss or pain, or maybe both. "Where the hell is he from anyway?"

Ignoring her brother, she kept her gaze focused on Graham.

"I don't understand," she repeated, recognizing the anger—knew it was directed at her—but between his foreign words and lack of explanation, she remained in the dark.

Alone.

"I found the chastity belt you discarded. The one you didn't want me to inspect too closely."

Her cheeks flamed while her brother lifted his bleeding head.

"You half-faced varlet." Hugo tried to stand, but he wavered on his feet and sank back to the bench. "How dare you insult my sister?"

Unable to harden her heart totally to her brother, Linnet placed a soothing hand on his back, feeling quite unsteady herself. Who would have thought she'd be siding with one of her hateful brothers on anything?

She walked unsteadily to the tub to dab a clean linen in the water so she might wash off Hugo's cuts.

"Why would you think I didn't want you to see the belt, Graham?" She would not be embarrassed in front of him after all they'd shared. Her brother looked too weak to take on Graham anyway. "It was my body that I hoped to hide from you at first, not some villainous piece of steel."

Hugo groaned as she washed the worst gash on his forehead, but she sensed he reacted more to the intimate discussion than the pain.

"You didn't want me to see the belt in case I discovered any clues about its origin. You didn't get locked into this belt in the twelfth century like you'd have me believe." Graham shook his head, disbelief scrawled across his brow as he made a sweeping gesture around the room. "All this is a lie. The castle we escaped from, the knights, the swords...all fake."

Hugo snickered. "'Tis he you should be tending, woman. Your friend has lost his wits."

Linnet plunked her wet linen on the table, assuming Hugo could care for himself if he possessed such a wealth of humor while her heart beat in fearful agitation and more than a little anger.

"I don't know what you accuse me of, Graham. My brother—beef-witted measle that he is—can attest to the time I was clamped in that belt."

"Artless wench," Hugo protested, as water dripped into his eye from the cloth he'd slapped to his head. "When did you grow such a sharp tongue?"

"I don't give a rat's ass what your brother has to say. Your so-called torturous chastity belt is neatly stitched with a notice inside that reads Made in Taiwan." Graham fumed in the middle of the hall, his hand tightening on the hilt of his sword. "That's all the proof I need to know you've all been lying to me. Why? I don't know. Maybe you've drugged me up like Kendrick's women and I've been imprisoned in some rural training camp for the Guardians' organization the last few days. I just need you to point me in the direction of L.A. and I'll be gone."

His words hit her like small stones, each one making her flinch a little more until she could scarcely bear to stand tall in front of him.

"Drugs? You mean herbs? Poisons?" Anger choked her along with the injustice of his accusations. "I cooked you a tottering hare, sir, and if you think I served it to you with poisons, you only have yourself to thank since you killed the beast."

Her feet started moving with the anger she felt and she was overcome by the need to be away from him before the hurt set in and the tears flowed. She felt them rise in her throat like a hot tide as she gestured out the open door.

"And as for your L.A.?" She had no idea what he meant, but that didn't stop her from pointing south into the sunny afternoon and a distant tree line. "You may find it if you proceed this way, sir. This way also lies a large body of water you may gladly jump in and—I sincerely hope—hell itself."

GRAHAM THOUGHT ABOUT LEAVING. The sun had not set yet thanks to the long days of Midsummer. And if he believed for a minute that Los Angeles rested south of here, he would have sprinted away from the Welborne siblings while Linnet went to tend to her oafish brother who'd shown up looking like the walking dead.

But when she'd been pointing out the door, Graham

had recalled that the sun didn't even set on the correct side of the water here—wherever here might be. So Linnet couldn't have been lying to him about that.

And now that some of his initial fury had worn off and he'd seen firsthand her reaction to his accusations, Graham had to wonder what else she hadn't been lying about.

He watched where she tended her brother, her movements efficient and graceful despite the floor-length gown she wore. As if she'd been wearing that kind of gown her whole life.

His heart hurt to look at her—he couldn't deny that was part of the reason his anger had turned into a flash fire instead of a slow simmer he might have hidden.

He was about to ask her a more civilized question about the chastity belt when the rumble of thunder sounded in the distance.

"Kendrick approaches!" Hugo shouted, scrambling away from Linnet to bar the door Graham had refused to walk through. "You'll take cover if you have any sense, man. Especially if you're the lack wit who broke her free of her future husband's claim."

While Graham tried to process why Linnet and her brother would try to perpetuate a lie Graham had already called them on, Hugo pulled Linnet deeper into the fortification toward a round tower room in the center of the structure. He shoved her inside while he pulled out a quiver full of arrows and two longbows.

Did Hugo make all that effort for Graham's benefit? The hint of fear in the other man's eyes suggested otherwise.

Once the two men heard her footsteps disappearing up to the second floor of the tower, Graham turned to the brother while Hugo tugged the weaponry to the walls.

"What the hell did you come here for anyhow?" Graham peered out the slits to see five riders closing in on the dwelling.

"'Tis my house, little lordling, and don't be forgetting it." The oaf pointed a finger in Graham's face. "And she's my sister. I never felt good about locking her up, but I was outvoted two to one in our family, and we stick together."

"So why did you lead Kendrick right to her if you're so concerned for her safety?"

"I didn't lead them here." He wiped a trickle of sweat off his brow, leaving a dirt smudge on the fresh bandage Linnet had given him. "I came to warn her that Kendrick came back and he's determined to find her. When he arrived at Welborne Keep to discover her gone, he beat the daylights out of all of us."

"You're suggesting the man who sought to marry Linnet did this to you?" Graham eyed the guy. He really did look like death warmed over.

"He's ruthless. He told us the only reason he didn't kill us right then was so we would help him find her." Hugo took up position in one of the arrow slits and threaded a longbow with an arrow he'd dragged from the tower room. "I knew she'd come here because she's always liked this place. Don't ask me why, since her mother died here."

It seemed a surreal conversation to discuss Linnet's mother while firing arrows out the fortification, but that's exactly what they did. Graham might be an expert with a sword, but his shot went wild, earning him a snicker from Hugo.

The oaf, in the meantime, took down one of the guys riding shotgun. Really took him down. As in dead.

These guys weren't playing.

Whether or not Graham wanted to believe he'd been hanging out in medieval England this week, he had to admit the battle being carried out now was all too real. And whether or not Linnet had lied to him, she was in serious danger.

A fact that moved him quickly past any residual anger to acknowledging he'd still never let anything happen to her.

Swallowing his pride and possibly a small amount of stupidity, Graham readjusted the longbow on his shoulder and turned to the oaf for help while the four riders picked up speed.

"So what's the trick with these weapons?"

LINNET FUMED IN THE UPSTAIRS tower room, too hurt and angry to be scared of her enemy's arrival just yet.

Graham thought she'd lied about…everything? She didn't understand his accusations, and that upset her. After all they'd shared, didn't she deserve more than him retreating to full use of his confusing language? And how dare he not explain why he thought it a grievous sin her loathed metal belt had been crafted in the land called Taiwan?

How did that take away from the pain of being a prisoner in her own keep? A prisoner in her own body?

Unwilling to be a pawn in games of masculine domination any longer, she marched down the tower steps to fight beside her brother and claim her fate as her own. As frustrated as she might be with Graham right now, she had to admit he'd given her the confidence to stand up for herself. Wherever he came from, the women must be very strong creatures, an ideal she now embraced wholeheartedly.

And now, after overhearing Hugo's tale of brutality at Kendrick's hands, Linnet decided if Kendrick besieged the fortification and won, at least she would know she'd fought for herself, which was more than she'd done in the past.

She'd been a fool to sit docilely around Welborne Keep for three years and wait patiently for a hated marriage. Graham Lawson may have taught her about betrayal and heartbreak, but at least being with him had opened her eyes to strengths she'd never known she possessed. Hadn't she walked many miles in the dark to escape Welborne Keep? She'd scaled a narrow plank to reach a second-floor balcony. Escaped a maniac intent on doing her harm by proving as slippery as a fish in a crisis. And she'd chosen a beautiful moment of her own for initiation into womanhood instead of waiting passively for a well-known rutting beast to wrest away her virginity in a moment of tears and pain.

Plucking up the smallest sword from the chest of armor at the end of the tower stairs, Linnet emerged from her hiding place to see Graham's sinews straining as he pulled the bowstring of his weapon into firing position.

Cursing the predictable feminine response to seeing a fine warrior utilize his considerable strength, she tugged her gaze away from Graham to see Hugo lick the feathers of an old arrow to improve its flight.

"What the hell are you doing down here, girl?"

"My God-given name is Linnet," she corrected her brother, knowing she'd picked a ridiculous time to become prickly about manners, but sometimes enough was enough.

This happened to be one of those times.

Out the narrow slit, she could see Graham's arrow had found its mark in the thigh of Kendrick's second in command, a whey-faced weasel of a man who'd accompanied Kendrick for the sennight he'd spent at Welborne Keep.

"You need to get in the tower. Now." Graham did not even bother to turn and look at her, his gaze trained out the second arrow slit as he spoke.

"You need to keep your own counsel now," she retorted, although she lost some of her steam as she watched Burke Kendrick take a flaming torch from one of his men and approach the door to the fortified house.

"Shit." Graham grabbed a fistful of arrows and hefted the longbow on his shoulder before he seized her elbow and shoved her none-too-gently back into the tower room.

Back up the staircase she'd just descended.

"You cannot call me ten kinds of liar and then decide you rule me at the same time." She spun on him in the middle of the staircase and then nearly fell backward when he practically marched right over her.

"Holy hell, will you come on?" He wrenched her to her feet again, his touch feeling far too delicious for a man she should resent.

"I'm not going anywhere until you explain why it is so bad to be made in Taiwan."

He massaged his temples with one hand and picked her up under his other arm.

"I've got arrows to rain on a certain man's head before he breaks in and kills your brother. God only knows what he'll do to you." Stomping up the stairs with a longbow over his shoulder and carrying her, too, Graham shoved his way into the second-floor tower room and set her down.

As she smelled smoke from the flaming arrows or—God forbid—the front entrance burning down, she heeded Graham's advice. She couldn't risk Hugo's life after he'd attempted to warn her of this very disaster.

Dusting herself off, Linnet shouted down the stairs to her brother.

"There is a washtub by the hearth, Hugo!" Guilt pinched her as she realized she should have been preparing the holding for battle instead of indulging her own hurts. "Douse the door."

"'Twill be a simple task once yer lover's blasted arrows start coming so I can— Nice shot."

She realized Graham was at work with the longbow out one of the arrow slits, his movements quick and efficient as he strung a new shaft in his weapon.

"They're backing off the walls now," Graham

shouted back to her brother. "I'll make sure they don't get close again."

Linnet heard the sizzle of water dousing flames and hoped Hugo had saved the door before it weakened too much. She moved to peer out the arrow slit across the round chamber from where Graham stood, but her slipper caught on the strap of a traveling satchel not unlike her own.

Curious, she picked up the sack to find it crammed full of her own belongings—gowns, tapestries, jewels, plates.

"What is this?" she asked herself more than Graham since she didn't expect him to know.

"Didn't you notice your brother drag in a bag with him when he arrived at your door?" Graham's eyes flicked over her briefly before returning to his quarry on the ground below. "He stashed it up here before he saw Kendrick coming."

"He brought me my things?" Her throat closed with the realization that her younger brother had taken such a risk.

"Anything else made in the Orient?" Graham's words, while disgruntled, lacked the venom they'd held earlier.

"That is where your Taiwan is located? The Far East?"

He lounged against the stone wall near the arrow slit overlooking half the lands.

"Yes, ma'am. Taken any trips abroad lately? Post-industrial Age?"

He spoke in nonsense again, clearly still angry even if he hadn't taken the opportunity to walk away when she'd offered it. Although, now that she thought about it, thank the saints he had not left then or he could have been killed when Kendrick and his men rode in unexpectedly. No matter how deep her hurt or sense of betrayal, the tenderness she felt for Graham remained. Indeed, she feared her feelings only grew the longer she stayed with him.

Still her champion, even through his fury with her. Albeit, a champion who spoke in riddles.

Even now he fought for her. And although one of her three brothers seemed to have shaken off his drunkenness enough to try and make amends to her for his past abuses, Hugo's remorse for his actions would certainly have come too late if she'd not broken free of Welborne Keep in the first place and given Kendrick a reason to beat the Welborne men. If not for Graham, she would have been lost to the monster in the courtyard.

"I have not taken any journeys recently, as I believe I mentioned to you that I have been a prisoner in my own home for three years." She smiled sweetly at Graham, refusing to be daunted by the dark cloud perched over his head.

He had fought for her, even when he had not known her or if her cause was just. So she would fight for him now, even when his faith in her had been shaken for reasons she didn't understand.

When he said nothing, she dug deeper into the satchel stuffed full of her possessions.

"But if you are so skilled at recognizing work from the Orient, perhaps you would glance at a tapestry I purchased from a wizened little peddler a few years ago.

He had the most extraordinary hair sticking out of his cap at all angles." She found her tapestries rolled up together—only three of the many that hung around Welborne Keep, but these were her favorites that had adorned her bedchamber. "He swore this one piece was crafted by skilled hands from the Far East, but I fear he only meant to drive up the price."

Whatever Graham had been about to say was lost in a sudden flurry of movement from beside the arrow slit as he yanked his bow arm back for another shot and shouted at the top of his lungs.

"Incoming!"

Scrambling to her feet, Linnet ran to the other narrow opening only to see Kendrick and his three remaining men gallop hard and fast toward the holding with a log poised for a battering ram.

14

GRAHAM DROPPED HIS BOW and grabbed a sword after his last shot took out one more of Kendrick's crew. As the oak door splintered with a loud crack under the weight of the barrier, Graham should have felt comforted that the odds were only three to two now.

But something about Kendrick's kamikaze fighting style, pushing his objective no matter how many men he lost in the process, gave Graham a bad feeling about this confrontation.

"By all that's holy, Linnet, stay here. Bar the door behind me and do not open it until I come for you."

Her green eyes were huge and he hated to leave, but the door below cracked further and he could not allow Hugo to fight alone in his weakened condition. Come to think of it, with Hugo all battered from a recent ass kicking, perhaps the odds were more like three to one and a half.

Plowing through the downstairs door of the tower and into the great hall, Graham found Hugo waving his sword wildly over the fractured entrance to the holding, his arm obviously weak. If Graham had made it to his side a few seconds sooner, he might have stopped the enemy surge, but a sword from without got hold of Hugo's sword and flung it backward, clearing the path to enter.

Graham engaged the first man through the door, a man whose face he remembered from the woodland T & A show the night before. With pleasure, Graham swiped his blade with dizzying speed.

"I see you're less of a threat when your opponents aren't naked women," Graham taunted, not above using a little old-school playground warfare to tick off his enemy and help his cause.

He had the guy on the run, the other man blocking blows as he walked backward. Graham kept coming, focused. Pissed.

Until a loud voice shouted over the clatter of swords.

"Halt or your comrade gets his throat slit."

Comrade?

Graham's thoughts raced as he halted. Wasn't that a newer term than medieval language allowed, or was he imagining things? His knowledge of word origins sucked and he was admittedly paranoid since the incident with Linnet's belt. A gift from Kendrick, now that he thought about it.

Turning, he relinquished his upper hand in the battle, knowing he could have had the guy unarmed with one more minute. His timing had been off all day.

Kendrick's other knight held Hugo by the head. Hugo was on his knees, his cut reopened in the struggle, his battered body now covered with soot from the fire he'd doused.

Damn. Graham raised one hand in surrender while he lay his sword on the nose of the battering ram that still rested the threshold to the holding. No sooner had he relinquished the piece than the snot-nosed knight he'd fought into a corner wrenched the blade out of Graham's reach.

Ignoring Kendrick's men, Graham focused solely on the ringleader whom so many feared.

"No need to hurt the young Welborne. He wants his sister back as badly as you do." The lie probably wouldn't work, but it was worth a shot to give Hugo a break. "He came here ready to tear the place apart but he, too, had to admit she is no longer under his rule."

Kendrick's muscles twitched beneath the dull gleam of a chain-mail shirt.

"Yet the youngest Welborne hardly welcomed me inside your little rat's nest this afternoon, so I can't consider him my ally, either."

Kendrick's dark zealot's eyes shone, his grip on his blade noticeably tightening as he joined his fellow knight in threatening Hugo.

"But I'm the only one who knows for certain where Linnet went."

"This you will tell me, or you will find both your throats slit."

"Dead men tell no tales though, right?" Graham had never gone in for the psych applications of police work, but his gut instinct told him to needle Kendrick if he wanted to buy time.

Stay alive.

"They might if they want their death to be quick and painless as opposed to agonizing and slow." He arced his sword back and forth a heart-stopping moment. Graham thought the zealot was going to make good on his threat to kill Hugo, but at the last minute he pulled the blade and simply cold-cocked him in the temple enough to knock him into next year.

Freeing Kendrick to stalk closer, his sword at his side but still in his hand, ready. The other man who'd first grabbed Hugo watched over the fallen man now, keeping a dagger pointed at his neck, no doubt to keep Graham in line more than any fear Hugo would come out of it any time soon.

"You know, I think I'd actually prefer the agonizing route since I'd have the comfort of knowing you couldn't even keep track of one woman when you had three warriors to watch over her and a steel cage to lock her in."

"You find that amusing?" Kendrick's breath smelled of onions and stale beer as he closed in on Graham.

Close enough to attempt intimidation but not close enough for a dropkick. A damn shame considering how badly the guy needed to be beaten senseless.

"Yeah, I do. But I think you misjudged the fighting spirit of medieval women when you went off and left her for years on end." Graham felt a sword in his back, no doubt at the behest of his host who seemed to dole out little mind-control orders to his last remaining men without even engaging in normal conversation.

"They are usually easier to predict than modern

women, I've found. But apparently I made a mistake with Linnet, who possesses an unusual amount of fire."

Graham might have informed him exactly how much fire she possessed that Kendrick would never know, but Graham was still struggling to believe his ears. Had Kendrick really just conversed about the differences between medieval and modern women? Something he'd only know if he was part of a modern cult intent on re-enacting the Dark Ages, or…

If Kendrick himself was a time traveler.

"Why target women with the Sight?" Graham's neck prickled in warning as he acknowledged that, somehow, Burke Kendrick might play a very direct role in the Guardians' abductions and flesh peddling taking place in L.A. along with the crimes Graham and Linnet had witnessed on Midsummer.

"I owe you no explanations if you have not put the pieces together by now on your own." Kendrick raised his sword, but at the same time he pulled a smaller knife out from the belt at his waist. "But I seem to remember I *do* owe you some agony, do I not?"

Graham gauged the room and the moment, knowing without Hugo, his three-to-one odds sucked all the more with no weapon in sight at his disposal. But then, swords were his specialty.

Before he could match footwork with the cape-wearing dudes in chain mail, however, the door to the tower burst open and Graham's heart seized up tight in his chest.

Linnet stood there with an arrow in her hand that she let rip free as if she were throwing a javelin.

"I'm sorry, Graham." She shot him a pleading look as one of Kendrick's guys rushed her—grabbed her—and the other dropped to his knees after taking the pointed tip of her arrow in his temple. "But I cannot honor your request not to interfere when it means you might be harmed on my behalf."

He wanted to save her, to reclaim her, but Kendrick's sword prevented him from making a move just yet. Graham's heart stopped seizing at that moment and broke wide open for the woman he never should have doubted. She was willing to confront her worst nightmare for Graham. A fact that only proved she wouldn't have lied to him about the chastity belt or about her belief that she lived in 1190.

Now that he finally understood the nature of the dangers they faced, he only hoped it wasn't too late to save her from an enemy unlike any he'd ever encountered. His heart filled with love for her just as Kendrick's sword swiped through the air to land on the back of Graham's head.

Knees buckling beneath him, Linnet's terrified screams were the last thing he heard.

"YOU SCUM-SUCKING BASTARD!" Linnet rushed toward the place where Graham had fallen.

"Best to leave him be, my sweet." Kendrick caught her in his arms, his knives sheathed for the moment while his one remaining knight kept blades trained on both her brother and her lover, one in each hand. "I hear head wounds are a bitch if you move the victim at all. I'd hate to see your champion suffer more permanent damage."

She knew the pain knifing through her heart must rival the physical agony Graham had felt when Kendrick's sword had struck his head. But she hadn't entered the fray to fight with her might. She had defied Graham's edict that she stay put because she had no choice other than to battle Kendrick with wits.

"You had better pray that he is not permanently damaged or I will never share my visions with you and provide the knowledge you seek." She prayed Graham had interpreted Kendrick's motives correctly as she used the tactics Graham had shown her on their ride to the Midsummer debacle. He'd intimidated his enemy through believable threats.

A tactic that had to work since she had not thought beyond this small show of force.

Kendrick's arm loosened just enough to spin her toward him so they stood facing in an angry, strenuous embrace.

"I will hurt you in ways you cannot yet imagine if you do not deliver the information I seek." He had changed in the last three years, the planes of his face hardening, the way he commanded a room growing more dramatic and absolute.

Linnet had the sense that he could have her killed—or have Graham killed—with no more than a nod of his head.

A shiver of fear froze on its way up her spine but she did not give it any outlet lest he know she was feeling outmaneuvered at this strategic game. She would not let Graham down again.

"That only shows how little you know about human caring. Why would I care that you hurt me when my lover is more important to me than myself?" She waited for him to strike her at the blatant admission of her relationship with Graham, but although her enemy's grip tensed and his face went first white and then red, Kendrick did not use physical force just yet.

"You care so little about your ability with the Sight that you would risk diminishing it by spreading your legs for a man?"

His voice was a frigid whisper, his accusation full of disgust. She braved a glance toward Graham to strengthen her resolve.

And dear God, had he just moved or had she only seen what she wanted to see? She did notice that the warrior knight who guarded Graham observed Kendrick and Linnet with more interest than the unconscious man.

Finally, a bit of good fortune.

"I diminish nothing," she scoffed, pretending a knowledge she did not possess. "Whoever told you that physical intimacy ruined such powers?"

Kendrick relinquished his hold on her, perhaps in part because of his obvious fury toward her.

"My mother was renowned for her ability to see the future. She confided everything I need to know about the art of scrying and foretelling."

"Fortune-telling is not the same as having the Sight." She thought she could see Graham moving a little more out of the corner of her eye so she purposely walked in the other direction to draw his guard's eye away. "Besides, how could consummation hurt a woman's ability with the Sight if your own *mother* boasted facility with her power after she bore a child?"

"Are you suggesting my mother gave me false information?" His gaze narrowed along with the other man's who was supposed to be guarding Graham.

Linnet would not have noticed the other man except that Graham reached toward the hem of his captor's cape and held a tiny blue canister beneath the fabric. With the flick of Graham's thumb, a small orange flame leaped from the blue vial.

"I am certain your mother knew her powers well." She did not look toward the oblivious guard, and readied herself to take action. "But perhaps every seer likes to maintain an element of mystery about what makes her abilities special."

An unholy scream tore through the chamber as the knight realized he was on fire, or at least his cape went up in flames. The unfortunate man did not seem to know the difference judging by the ruckus he raised as he tore through the great hall in circles.

"Hold your man," Kendrick shouted at his burning knight.

Graham swiped the blazing man's sword with ease and wielded it toward Kendrick while Linnet backed against the safety of the tower wall, which was well beyond Kendrick's reach.

"If ever there was an opportune moment to journey through time, buddy, now would be it." Graham leveled his sword at Kendrick's heart while the burning man flung himself in what little water remained in the washtub still sitting near the hearth.

The hiss of burned cloth and singed hair filled the chamber along with the man's wails of pain.

"So you've learned the truth, Detective." Kendrick clutched his own sword, though it remained low by his side. A position of weakness compared to Graham's dominant stance.

"Your preference for toys made in Taiwan clued me in." Graham must have pushed on the sword tip slightly since Kendrick flinched. "Thanks for the dumb-ass mistake. Makes my job so much easier."

Linnet listened in disbelief and confusion. Kendrick had made the terrible Taiwan mistake and not her? She did not understand their conversation about journeying through time but she began to suspect Kendrick hailed from the same foreign land as Graham.

"I find anachronism amusing," Kendrick shrugged, albeit carefully, in deference to Graham's blade. "I don't see where it's much of a mistake when you haven't even begun to suspect the nature of my kidnappings or the ways I've amassed my wealth."

Linnet picked up a loose rock from the floor that must have crumbled away from the walls when the battering ram had broken through the door. She would be ready to act when the moment was right or when Kendrick attempted an escape.

"You steal women for their extrasensory perception." Graham reached into a pouch at the back of his braies with one hand and pulled out the blue vial he'd used to set the other knight on fire. "Those who don't show enough aptitude are sold as sex slaves."

"You make it sound so sordid. And I don't sell them all. I give some away to my knights—or my most loyal gang members, depending on the century—as reward for services rendered."

"What does he mean?" Linnet gripped her rock for protection, unable to stay quiet any longer when clearly the men understood one another far better than she understood either one of them.

"You haven't told her?" Kendrick smiled a dark and wicked grin even though he never took his attention away from Graham. "How dishonorable of you when you were born to protect and serve."

"Your ex-boyfriend travels through time committing crimes," Graham informed her. "He hasn't been on Crusade the last three years. He's been in twenty-first-century L.A. setting up another gang of screwed-in-the-head neophytes to do his dirty work."

Graham flicked on the blue canister, igniting a small flame that he waved threateningly close to Kendrick's cape while Linnet tried to process what he'd said.

"L.A. That is where you are from." She remembered their first conversation. Graham Lawson LAPD. Was he really a traveler through time as well?

The notion was preposterous. Was it not?

An overwhelming sense of betrayal made her knees

weak as she wavered on her feet. Had she been an inconvenience on Graham's path to justice?

Or worse, a conduit to find Kendrick in 1190? She remembered with damning clarity how Graham had asked her to tell him the date that first night in her bedchamber.

"Setting up the gangs is the least of it," Kendrick sneered, ignoring her in favor of bragging to Graham. "Harnessing the women's powers to uncover treasures all over the world is the fun part. Perhaps my next target should be the Sex Through the Ages exhibit. A fitting end to our battles, wouldn't you say, Lawson?"

Linnet's gut roiled in protest at the thought of Kendrick's crimes that she was only just beginning to understand. Half of her wished Graham would simply run him through and have done with it. But just then, Kendrick's image started to…fade?

One moment he was there, flinching from the nick of the sword's edge and the next moment the edges of his rangy body grew fuzzy. Dim.

"I am only sad it will not be Linnet who leads me to the next treasure." His ghostly, half-present self looked over his shoulder at her while everyone else in the chamber gawked at the spectacle.

Graham attempted to run him through at that moment but he fell into air, his sword meeting no resistance. Still, they could hear Kendrick's voice as if from far away.

"Thankfully, I have a couple of college coeds who can't wait to serve me on my next endeavor."

Linnet was certain her mouth hung wide open as she

gaped at the place where a monstrous man had stood only moments ago.

"Damn it!" Graham launched into a string of obscenities that even her brothers had probably never matched.

Hugo finally stirred at the commotion while the injured knight hurried toward the cracked-open chamber door to escape into the night.

"Holy hell." Hugo shook his head as if to clear it while Graham swung his sword in a vicious arc of empty air. "You must have the devil's own sword arm to have saved the day all by yourself."

Linnet shook her head at the two of them, her heart well and truly broken thanks to Graham's lies. Bad enough when he had not believed her when she'd told the truth. But for him to point fingers at her character when he'd been lying to her all along?

"The day has not been saved, brother. It has been lost with lies," Linnet assured him as she mourned the man she'd grown to care for. He had disappeared as surely as Kendrick had faded into nothingness.

Worse, the Graham Lawson she'd thought she knew had never existed at all.

15

HOW MANY WAYS COULD A MAN screw himself over?

Graham figured if Guinness gave out a world record for longest string of devastating errors, he'd have a lock on the category. He'd lost his bad guy in two different centuries, unleashed a sexual predator on two unsuspecting women in present-day L.A., blamed Linnet for lying to him when the fault lay solely with the ex-fiancé she'd told him all along was no good and now on top of it all he had to explain why he hadn't bothered confiding the truth of his origins to her before now.

He tore his gaze off the darkened courtyard where he must have decided to search for signs of Kendrick at some point during the bout of recrimination.

"Linnet?" Turning toward the hall interior, Graham sought her out in the chamber full of shadows as twilight turned to full darkness.

"She went up the tower steps a moment ago," Hugo provided, a quiet presence next to Graham's simmering fury. "Shall I ride out to look for any sign of him?"

"A man who vanished into thin air?" He couldn't even wrap his brain around the physics of time travel, let alone a man who could make it happen at will. "Don't bother. And thank you for coming back for Linnet. I know that having you here meant a lot to her."

Hugo lit a fire in the hearth, a spark popping anew as he stirred the ashes of a flame Graham had thought long dead.

"It occurred to me that it was never too late to atone for a past wrong. No matter whether she forgave me or not, I needed to at least admit I made a mistake to hurt her." The guy's brawny shoulders seemed straighter than Graham remembered when he'd last met the guy at Welborne Keep, arguing about the proper way to infuse a spit wad with extra flight power.

"Are you trying to tell me something?"

"Who me?" Hugo tossed another piece of wood on the growing blaze. "I'm just tending the home fire and wishing I didn't have so many regrets."

Rising to his feet, he clapped Graham on the shoulder and limped toward the door.

"Tell Linnet if she needs me, I'll be outside keeping watch for that milksop varlet I nearly forced her to marry."

Straightening, Graham figured he'd better start tending a home fire of his own. Because if there was any chance he could explain away his actions or make her understand why he'd kept the truth of his past to himself…

Well, he'd be an idiot not to try.

Taking the tower stairs two at a time, he raced up to the room he'd locked her in to keep her safe. Instead, she'd kept him safe, probably kept him alive by telling

Kendrick she wouldn't cooperate if the jerk-off hurt Graham. Or at least, that's what Graham dreamed had happened. But he couldn't be sure what he'd dreamed and what had really happened when he'd been unconscious on the great hall floor earlier.

Reaching the second floor of the tower, he pushed open the door that remained half-open. Linnet crouched on the floor, a candle beside her as she gazed at a huge tapestry she'd unrolled to cover half the small chamber.

A tear glistened in her eye as she seemed lost in the view, but Graham could not care about the picture when his every instinct screamed to fix this, to make sure that tear didn't roll down her soft cheek.

"I'm so freaking sorry." He dropped down on one knee beside her, careful not to crowd her but needing to be closer. "Linnet, I don't even know where to begin with all the things I'm sorry for."

"You traveled through time to stop Kendrick." Her voice remained strong and clear and more than a little pissed off despite the sheen of wetness in her eye.

"Maybe. Probably. I don't know, actually, because it wasn't a conscious decision." He relayed the facts of the episode as succinctly as possible from his investigation that had taken him to the exhibit, to his fall through the painting and ultimate arrival in her closet. "I didn't even know for sure what had happened to me. I kept thinking I was part of a movie—it's a kind of dramatic entertainment in the twenty-first century. Like a play."

"You thought I was an actress. A player. Even though I remember telling you quite clearly that I did not play a game." She tucked her gown around her legs and sat cross-legged on the floor, her candle still flickering softly in the darkness and painting ominous shadows all over the round room.

"I didn't know what to believe, but I did come to believe you." Yet he hadn't shown faith in her. He could almost hear the words she did not speak. "Then when I saw the belt had come from another time period, I was angry at myself for having— Damn it, Linnet, you didn't deserve my distrust but I find it next to impossible to believe people without some kind of evidence to back it up."

"Why?" She did not plead her case or yell; she simply pushed the matter when he hadn't explained to her satisfaction.

He could hardly blame her.

A shaft of moonlight suddenly filtered in through one of the arrow slits, brightening the chamber.

"Remember how you asked me who—uh—hurt me in the past?" He didn't want to tell her any of the stupid points of his history that only made him sound like a whiner in his mind. But he couldn't look himself in the eye ever again if he didn't make every effort to fix things with her.

With the woman he loved.

Renewed confidence filled him as he reminded himself that tending the home fire wasn't always about setting the big-ass blaze to light the rest of the world. Sometimes you had to admit your spark sucked and take a little warmth from somebody else. He could deal, couldn't he? Share something that sucked so Linnet could at least understand him better?

And hell, if she wanted to spread a little warmth his way after all the ways he'd hurt her, he'd count his blessings a million times over.

"I remember." Linnet ran her fingers over the weave of the tapestry.

"I guess I'm fairly cautious about who I let get close to me after an incident as a kid where an abusive son of a bitch played the nice-guy stepfather to me and won me over before I realized what he was doing to my mom." That grudge was still going strong, but the guilt outweighed it by double.

"Many men are abusive," Linnet assured him, her fingers slowing to trace the leaves of a tree stitched into the heavy fabric. "But I agree that there is something all the more devastating about a man who hits and yet wears a charming face. Were you hit as well?"

"No. I think maybe I could have handled the guilt better if I had been. Or at least I would have known what a monster this guy could be."

"You are fearful of being fooled the same way I am fearful of being locked away—or worse—alone."

He reached to stroke her hair, hoping this wouldn't be the last time he touched her.

"Linnet, I have to go back to my home. I have no choice. But you can come with me. I *want* you with me. Hell, I'm not going to leave your side unless you ask me to." He wasn't sure if the time was right to admit he loved her, even though he knew it deep in his soul already. She was young and she'd been through so much. Way too much to take on his baggage as well.

"I am not certain I want to be with a man who doubts me so deeply he cannot share anything about his home. His past. His life's journey. I find I don't know you at all."

"Yes, you do." He had no choice but to touch her now, to pull her into his arms and remind her how well they knew one another. "You know me better than anyone because I've been more myself here, with you, than I've been in a long time."

The scent of her, of her soap that he'd personally lathered over her skin, made him crazy with memories. With want.

"I don't understand." She paused in her tapestry tracing to look at him, her head shaking in confusion.

And she didn't believe him—he could see it in her eyes.

"I moved three thousand miles last year to be with a woman I thought I cared about only to find out I was a useful stepping stone for a bigger and better relationship for her. And that time, I really wasn't hurt, just mad at myself for not being true to what I really wanted in life. I'd become so antisocial before meeting my former girlfriend that she had to seek me out. Flirt with me." *Manipulate me.* He'd never wanted to work on the movie set, but he went a couple times a week to hang out with a bunch of Hollywood types because he'd felt obligated.

"Why do you think it is any different here? Why would you think I didn't seek you out? After all, you would have left Welborne Keep if I asked you to go. Instead, I attached myself with you and asked for help. Perhaps I…what did you say?…*flirt* with you as well?" She looked concerned about what nefarious crime flirting might be.

"Flirting isn't a problem. It's like…enticing talk." God, he prayed she'd want to flirt with him again one day. And kiss him. And make love to him in waterfalls. In front of fireplaces…

"But why do you think it is any better to be with me than a woman who forced you to be someone you are not?" Her lips pursed in a thoughtful pout. "You are not really a knight, after all. It seems to me, you are not yourself in this realm either."

"But I was born to wield a sword." He hadn't realized how fated it seemed that he come back in time to meet Linnet until just now, but he would have been dead by now if not for his lifelong interest in weaponry—swords in particular. "I am at home in this time in a way I'm not in Hollywood. And now I understand that whether or not I can convince you to come back with me to the twenty-first century, I need to move to the country, far away from pop culture and false faces."

He could tell by her wrinkled brow he had not said the right words. Damn it. They both spoke English, and yet their languages were so far apart.

"Linnet," he tried again. "With you, there is no artifice. Like you said, you don't play games. And I just hope with all my Johnny-come-lately heart that I haven't messed up my chance with a woman who's perfect for me just because I hail from a land of phony people and somehow wound up a cynic."

Her finger went back to tracing the lines of the tapestry, perhaps lost in thought as she weighed his words. The tension, the fear of losing her, clamped his heart so damn tightly he could only hold his breath and watch her fingernail scratch lightly along the curving stem of a grapevine beneath a mellow afternoon sun.

Grapevine?

Shoving to his feet, Graham changed his perspective on the tapestry for a bird's-eye view. He could hardly appreciate her decor when half-seated upon it, but from above, he recognized wine country that could be Italy, or perhaps…Napa Valley?

Holy hell.

"Remember you said something about a tapestry you purchased recently?" He grabbed her lit taper to hold it aloft for a better angle on the image. "Is this the one?"

A crazy idea formed in his head. A foolish idea. Full of risks that could land them in the middle of a vineyard during the American Revolution. Or the Italian Renaissance. Or God knows where. But all Graham had to go on now was instinct. And he just so happened to recall there was a vineyard or two around Santa Barbara. Not exactly a stone's throw from his place, but he'd be happy if they landed in the right state, let alone the right city.

"Aye." Linnet nodded. "I bought it from a peddler with crazy hair sticking out from his cap at all angles. He was insistent I should purchase it even though he asked a king's ransom in return."

Visions of the night watchman at the J. Paul Getty Museum returned. Had the old man known more about Graham's travel through time than Graham ever suspected?

"You were brilliant to buy it." He kissed her hard, pulling her against him for a fierce embrace with all the longing in his cagey, cynical, blind soul. "This picture is going to take us home if you'll let it."

HOPE AND FEAR DANCED seductively inside her, dodging and weaving, moving together in one seamless motion until she could not tell where one ended and the other began.

But she could not deny her fate any more than she could hurt the man who'd stolen her heart.

"I'm scared to leave—" What? The home where her drunken brothers held her captive? Who knew how long Hugo would remain sober. And as for a happy marriage or family, she would never have those things as long as Kendrick sought her. Besides, she began to think the only man she wanted to give her babes was the one who stood beside her now, his hand reaching out toward her....

"I will do everything in my power to make you at home. Buy you a house near a creek with a waterfall. Build a big-ass fence so no one sees you swimming naked. Except for me, of course, if you allow it." He stared at her with unwavering eyes, so sure of himself. "What do you say? Will you go with me?"

She started to reach for him, to take his hand and run toward whatever future they might share together, but the sound of crashing swords outside the holding made her hand freeze in midair.

Graham picked up her tapestry and rolled it under his arm before launching over to the arrow slit to peer down.

"Of all the blasted luck." He turned, an unlikely smile on his face. "Kendrick has returned with renewed forces and they seem to have engaged the Welborne clan."

Disbelief set her feet into high speed. And sure enough, Hugo, Douglas and John fought hand-to-hand with Kendrick's men in the courtyard. Her belated champions at last.

"They can't hold them for long," Graham assured her, reminding her the battle had not yet been won. Especially when one of the opponents could vanish into another time period by simply willing himself into nothingness.

"What do we need the tapestry for?" She carried a taper and followed him down the staircase, his sword in one hand and her favorite tapestry in the other.

"You wouldn't believe me if I told you, but I swear to you if you string that hanging between two trees while I help your brothers, you will see for yourself."

She thought she heard him mutter a halfhearted "I hope" as he tossed the heavy roll on the grassy lawn and ran into the fray with his sword already in motion.

How could she have ever doubted his warrior capabilities when he had once outsmarted her brothers, and twice helped her kinsmen to stay alive despite having sound reason to despise them? And no man on the field was Graham's equal with a sword. Only Burke Kendrick came close.

But Linnet noticed Graham dodged Kendrick's gaze with nimble-footed stealth, a feat assisted by the clouds gathered round the moon and the lack of torchlight in the courtyard around the fortification. She saw Graham engage an enemy, helping wounded Hugo defeat one of Kendrick's men.

Linnet dragged the heavy tapestry through patches of dew-damp grasses and flat stones, going about her work quietly in the shadows of the swordplay. Did twenty-first century women have to tiptoe around violence this way? Or had their men conquered some of their baser tendencies to keep the world a safer place?

Or…was the world safer because Graham Lawson—warrior for all time—protected his people in his role as sheriff?

The thought made her smile in spite of the clank of weaponry nearby. She prayed for her misguided kin and for Graham as she tied the silken cords around two tree trunks as he had requested. She'd just finished cinching a knot when strong, cold hands gripped her waist like grim death nipping at her heels.

She knew who held her without looking, and yet she could not reconcile herself that all her efforts to elude Burke Kendrick could still come down to this. She lurched forward, away from him, and a knife appeared at her throat.

"We will beat your lover to the future so you can join the other women who serve me," Kendrick whispered into her ear and she could not tell if her sudden vision of herself disappearing was a true experience of the Sight, or if she'd merely imagined her own worst fears.

"I will not go," she protested through clenched teeth out of deference to the blade at her throat. She strained her eyes to see Graham where her brothers fought an assortment of Kendrick's men.

"Oh, you will go." He squeezed her breast painfully with his free hand, digging deep beneath her surcoat to tweak the nipple. "And now that you have been despoiled, I hardly need to worry about protecting your skills with the Sight by saving your innocence. Rest assured I will be the next man to have you naked beneath me."

Fury for the women he'd brutalized gave her courage. Graham had shown her the honor in fighting for others who could not fight for themselves and, out here, she was no longer a docile prisoner of her own keep. She would give this bastard the battle of a lifetime.

Wrenching her knee forward, she kicked back like a donkey to plant her foot in his crotch, but she kicked only air as his hands, his body fell away from her.

She half fell on top of his fallen form before Graham's arms saved her, his sword clattering to the courtyard stones with a clank.

"You got him." She blinked in disbelief at the fallen man who'd terrorized her both waking and dreaming. Kendrick's body did not appear harmed from the front, but his eyes were already wide with death, his hand still clutching the knife he'd used to threaten her. His other hand gripped a handful of her kirtle she hadn't realized he'd torn.

"Are you okay? Jesus, Linnet, I had to take him out. Not just for you but for all the women he's stolen and sold into God knows what kinds of hellish slavery—"

"Frontier justice," she found herself whispering, recalling Graham's words about horses he'd commandeered from the bandits who'd beset him in the forest. "A quick death is a merciful end for a man whose deeds incited so much pain."

Graham squeezed her tighter and she was surprised to realize her words had offered him comfort. How fortunate was she to find a warrior with a heart? A conscience?

"Take me home with you, Graham." She didn't need to ask her stepbrothers for permission. They would fare well without her and she would pray for their souls in her absence. She would like to think they would find peace in restoring order to this part of the world in the king's absence. Maybe then they would find absolution for helping a wicked man.

Graham stepped back to peer at her in the darkness lit only by fickle moonlight.

"Are you sure?"

"We have others to save, do we not? Those other women Kendrick hurt need your aid as much as I have."

His hands cradled her head, tipping her face up to his so he could look into her eyes.

"I love you, Linnet. And you will be a free woman in my country to do whatever you want, even if that means you don't want to be with me. But I swear to you, no matter what you choose, I will never doubt you again and I'm damn well going to keep on loving you."

He kissed her until she saw stars, until the moon seemed to sink a bit lower in the sky, until her brothers defeated their foes to shout unseemly catcalls from across the courtyard.

She had a reply of love in her heart, but as soon as Graham released her, he called for his horse. And to her amazement, her oafish brothers delivered it along with Graham's fallen sword.

"You need to round up anyone wearing Kendrick's device now that he is dead," Graham told Hugo as he lifted Linnet up onto his horse's back.

"Aye." Hugo nodded and gestured toward the older men behind him who looked more haggard than she remembered, but more clear-eyed than she'd seen them in a long time. "And my kin have set a bonfire with the remains of the ale at Welborne. Seeing the brutality Kendrick was capable of made us all a bit wiser, I think."

Pity they couldn't have seen it long ago when she'd told them the same, but she could not begrudge them their belated attempts to make peace.

Graham dug in his braies to remove a black leather case. At first she thought he would take out another charmed bit of protection since that was the only time she could remember seeing the small case, but thankfully, he only removed a shiny gold brooch from the pouch, which Graham went on to affix to Hugo's surcoat.

"You are the sheriff of these lands now. It is your duty to protect and serve all who reside on it."

Hugo bowed low and even his older brothers looked properly humbled by the charge.

"Aye, my lord." He stood straighter with the gold emblem on his cloak. "Godspeed you both."

"Godspeed," Linnet whispered in return, her heart overcome to think Graham might have reformed the drunken oafs for good. "I wish you all well."

They hailed her health and long life as Graham climbed up onto the horse's back behind her. He tugged the reins to steer the mount toward...

The tapestry she'd hung?

"What are you doing?" She wondered if Graham had indulged in some spirits himself as he urged the horse forward at full speed.

"I'm praying that old man who sold you this tapestry is a friend of mine."

She had thought they would disappear into nothingness the way Kendrick had, but it appeared they would ride headlong through the tapestry. She screamed at the last minute, holding tight to Graham's neck as they hurtled into endless darkness.

16

LINNET AWOKE TO A SCENE she'd been staring at on the wall above her bed every night for the last year. Except this time, she didn't awake looking at the tapestry. She sat in a field full of tall grasses alongside a vineyard of rich green leaves and half-grown grapes. A mellow sunset disoriented her since it had been nighttime when she and Graham…

Graham.

Her hands already reaching to pat the ground beside her, she rose from her ungainly sprawl in the quiet field to see a horse grazing nearby and Graham lying a few feet away.

"Graham?" She crawled over to him, her head fuzzy with a mix of dreams and visions, past and present swirling through her brain. Was he all right?

A thunderous noise growled from overhead and scared a scream from her throat. She looked up to see a…metal bird?…hurtling above them at terrifying speed, a wake of white smoke filling the sky behind it.

"Welcome to the future, Lady Linnet." Graham's voice wrapped around her with soothing effect, settling her nerves into submission as she realized he was fine. Healthy. Whole.

And the tenderness in his eyes made her knees weak. She had so much she needed to say to him, but somehow words escaped her as she tried to take it all in.

"This is your homeland?" She began to notice subtle differences from the place she'd left. Tall poles in the distance held up thick wires. A shiny metal windmill stood taller than any building she'd ever seen on a nearby hillside.

"It feels more like home now that you're here." He levered up to a sitting position and plucked a leaf from her hair.

A ringing noise emanated from his braies and startled her all over again. The twenty-first century was noisy.

He reached into the pouch containing his magical knife and his fire-lighting device and pulled forth a metal object she'd not seen before. Covered in buttons, it lit up from within as it rang.

"I didn't miss cell phones, but I'll have to put a call in to my precinct as soon as we get you settled. And damned if this phone can't hold a charge." He clicked a button to make the ringing stop and then stared at her in the sudden quiet. "Would you have believed me if I tried to describe my homeland to you?"

Laughter bubbled up her throat. "Not in a million years would I have believed this. England looks very different in the twenty-first century."

"Oh. Um. Welcome to the New World. I can take you back to England sometime if you'd feel more at home there, but we're actually sitting on another continent that didn't get discovered by Europeans for three hundred years after you were born."

For a moment, the changes threatened to swallow her. But then Graham held her hands in his and she remembered why she'd braved this trip with him.

"I love you, Graham Lawson LAPD. And no matter how crazy your world feels to me right now, I know I'm going to grow to love this as my homeland, too, because you are here. Safety is here. And freedom is here." He'd given her so much more than love. He'd saved her. Inspired her. Made her want to be strong and brave like him.

Graham closed his eyes and kissed her as he wrapped Linnet in his heart as well as his arms. She felt soft and warm. Real.

And she loved him, too.

He couldn't begin to contemplate the miracles he'd witnessed in the last week, but somehow he'd explain the whole mess to his commanding officer. The disappearance. The capture of a criminal in another century—okay, he'd have to work on his delivery for that one—and the loss of his badge, which was a big freaking deal.

But no matter what came of it all, Graham had a new peace inside with Linnet in his life. She'd reminded him that love and loyalty coexisted. That life should be lived without guilt and fear. She'd be an inspiration at the local women's shelter if she ever decided to go that route and let her experience inspire others.

All that was in the future, however. Right now, he just

wanted to settle her somewhere safe until he could round up the rest of the Guardians and the women they held. He had a pretty good idea where to look since he still had Kendrick's scrolls with an inventory of his goods. He hadn't realized at first that some of the numbers along the bottom might be modern addresses, but once he'd discovered the guy traveled through time…the pieces had fallen into place.

"Are you ready for me to take you home?" He rose to his feet and held out a hand to her. Maybe they could take the horse if they stuck to back routes. No interstates for Buttercup.

"You have a keep near here?" She spun around to scan the landscape with her eye.

"It's more like a fortified house." Hey, he had a security system after all. "But I think we can be there in about an hour if we get moving."

He whistled to the mare that trotted over with reins dangling.

"Will we pass the holding of Lord Walmart on the way?" She grinned as she patted Buttercup's neck. "I think every woman in the twenty-first century should have a pocketknife."

"No doubt about it, but I don't know if you're ready for Wal-Mart today. It can be a bit overwhelming even for modern man." He helped her up on the horse's back, his hands fitting perfectly around her waist. "How about if I promise to take you tomorrow, but for tonight you come home with me and I'll show you a bath that remains hot at all times?"

"There really is such a thing?" Her eyes narrowed as he climbed up behind her.

He settled her across his lap, all too glad to undergo the delectable torture of her rump on his thighs when he would get to have her all to himself later tonight. And tomorrow. And tomorrow…

"One of many creature comforts I think you'll enjoy." He definitely needed to see about moving someplace with a waterfall in the backyard though. He couldn't wait to make new memories with her and relive some of his favorites so far.

Her cheeks turned a beautiful shade of pink and he wondered what she was thinking. He held the horse in check until he could find out.

"You look like a woman with something wicked on your mind."

Her hand brushed over his chest and dipped into the collar to touch bare skin.

"I was just remembering the charmed protection we used. You said it was from a medicine woman, but now that I see the wonders of your world, it occurred to me that—"

"That I might have been using a little twenty-first-century magic?" His body responded to the thought so damn fast he had no choice but to kick the horse in motion. Too bad he didn't have time to find a hotel on the other side of this vineyard, but duty called.

"Your guess is accurate and I know just where to find more of those charms." Not soon enough, damn it, but then he had a lifetime to explore those delights with

Linnet. "You've just discovered one of the greatest benefits of life in the modern age, sweetheart."

"I think I'm going to like it here," she whispered, unbuttoning his shirt to plant a kiss over his heart. "But I bet I will like it all the more if you can express to Buttercup my urgent need to be home if only so I can start waiting for your return to me."

"Aye, lady." He'd taken all week to acclimate himself to her language, but he thought he had this part right as he kicked the horse faster through the rolling fields and grapevines toward their future. "Your wish is my command."

Epilogue

One month later

"I SPENT EVERY CENT of my first check." Linnet plunked her shopping bags on Graham's kitchen table in the home they'd shared for the last month, thrilled to have joined the workforce a week ago so she could spend money that was all her own. She'd taken a temporary job at a large riding club just outside L.A. until she figured out what she wanted to do long term. Horses hadn't changed since her time and she savored the outdoor work that let her board Buttercup for free.

She would have gladly worked at Wal-Mart, having fallen in love with twenty-four-hour shopping even though she didn't know what to do with half the items sold there. A hunting rifle? Motor oil? Still, who wouldn't have fun playing with the rows and rows of ribbons in every color?

And then there were all the delectable candies.

But Graham had suggested she check out the university and that had proven as exciting as any Wal-Mart offering. She wanted to study—nay, major—in women's studies even though Graham said she would ace medieval history.

"You worked hard for your check," Graham assured her, wrapping his strong arms about her waist as he kissed her neck. "You deserve to spend it all."

She swished aside her shoulder-length hair, so light and freeing after years of caring for her waist-length mane.

"Hard work? I have a hot bath to start every day. No laundry to wash. No food to cook. My life is entirely too easy." Too wonderful. She still feared she would awake to discover it was all a dream, but Graham had assured her he'd often felt that way in her time, too.

Never could she return to the Middle Ages after discovering microwaves. Lights to brighten the bedchamber even at midnight in case you wanted to get a really good look at something. Or some*one*.

She loved every facet of her new life and appreciated Graham's patient, loving hand guiding her through this amazing new world. He'd offered to move out into the country to ease what he called "culture shock," but she'd flatly refused—for now, at least—since she savored the chance to see him in the realm that had made him such a wonderful man.

"I want to see everything you bought, but I have some news first." Graham sidled around her to face her, his silvery eyes serious. "We found the last of the Guardians today."

He'd worked so long and hard on his case since they'd returned. He'd quickly freed the women who'd been held by Kendrick's modern-day knaves after he'd returned to L.A. Apparently the device carved on Linnet's Initiator and sewn on Kendrick's banners had been a map of a local labyrinth imprisoned within the Guardians' stronghold and the women had been hidden within its depths. But after those triumphs, the investigation had halted when he'd failed to find a handful of key gang members named in the scrolls Graham had discovered.

"All three of them?" She'd listened to his anguish at not being able to locate those men, so she knew what a relief this had to be.

At his nod, she hugged him. Kissed his cheek.

They stood together in the middle of his kitchen in a house now decorated with tapestries he'd purchased to remind her of home and she let the love for him flow over her, the rightness of their union soothing the fears of her past.

"I knew you would." She liked to imagine her brothers had done the same thing in England after she'd left them; relentlessly rounding up Kendrick's followers to protect the women they sought to harm.

And, she prayed, without Kendrick's greed for gold gained with the Sight, perhaps his followers were not as driven without him to encourage them.

"These last few guys had some interesting insights on how Kendrick might have traveled through time. Not that they knew he could do that, but they gave up the information not knowing what it meant."

"I think he inherited the gift from his mother." Linnet

stood stubbornly by her theory as Lady Kendrick had been whispered to be a sorceress in her time.

"Perhaps, but it seems he didn't necessarily vanish into thin air. His cohorts say he was the David Copperfield of tricks like that." Catching himself, he explained. "That's a big-league magician in our time. Like a wizard, but the magic is just for show."

"But it couldn't have been just for show since we know he really traveled between times."

"Yeah, but him fading into nothingness was a little too *Star Trek* for my peace of mind. I think that was all a hoax to get himself out of a sticky situation and then he used a picture in his wallet to travel the same way we did." He pulled out a piece of paper that she now knew was a photocopy of another piece of paper.

Graham had photocopied her hand at his precinct and nearly scared ten years off her life.

"What is it?" She unfolded the paper and peered at a picture of a sleek, contemporary building.

"It's the J. Paul Getty Museum, the same place where I fell into the picture that led to you." Graham attached the paper to his icebox with a piece of plastic, and Linnet remembered him telling her that the Sex Through the Ages exhibit had moved from the Los Angeles museum to some far off city named Atlanta. "The guys we picked up today said Kendrick always carried pictures like this in his wallet. One of them claimed he had to make copies of pictures from all around the world—including a lot of historical sites—for Kendrick to keep in his billfold."

"And you think he pulled them out at whim and rode

into them just like we did?" She wondered idly if the curator of the Sex Through the Ages exhibit was pushing unsuspecting visitors into any pictures and long ago time periods during the show's visit to Atlanta.

"It's the best I can come up with." He shook his head even as he traced the line of her jaw with his thumb. "And now I find myself looking at people and wondering how many others are walking around having that kind of ability."

"We must celebrate." Linnet knew this was a landmark for Graham, who would always take his work seriously, no matter how much she encouraged him to play. And she loved that about him. Loved knowing he was out saving other people the way he'd saved her. Well, not *exactly* the way he'd saved her. "No microwave dinner tonight. I will cook for us myself."

Still not all that hard considering the freezer was bulging with food.

"You're incredible, you know that? You don't have to cook. You already shopped." A smile twitched at his lips before he pressed a kiss to the diamond engagement ring he'd placed on her hand a week ago. The claddagh design showed a heart within hands, an image that worked both ways for them.

"I have kept busy, haven't I?" She grinned in return, thinking the cooking could wait a few more minutes. "I don't know what's more fun, walking around a marketplace any day of the week I choose or discovering the endless wonders of Lycra. You'll never guess what I bought today."

She dug in the Victoria's Secret bag and came up with the prize she sought. It was black and lace and naughty and Graham was going to love it.

"It's a merry widow." His eyes were already crossing as he looked from the see-through fabric to her breasts, her hips.

He was truly too easy to please. And she would never grow tired of pleasing him. Or being pleased *by* him.

Her heart thudded harder at the thought.

"That's what the peddler said." She had so much to learn about Graham's time. Her time, now. But every day was an adventure she savored. "Don't you wonder why a widow should be so merry? What a peculiar name. Although I suppose I could Google it."

She adored her computer—Graham's computer that he'd all but given up to her after her endless questions about his world. Now she used Ask Jeeves and Google to find whatever she wanted to know. Of course, there were some things she still preferred Graham show her....

"I don't have a clue, but I can assure you, I'll make you damn well merry any time you care to wear this." He fingered the lace for a moment before casting it aside and pulling her into his arms. "God, I missed you today."

"I missed you, too." She stepped into his embrace, wondering how she'd gotten so lucky to have this noble, generous, sexy man in her life. "I thought I would grow more accustomed to sex any time we wanted it, but I fear I stopped by the Eckerd right after I left the market-place."

"More condoms?" He smiled through his kiss.

"Aye. Many, many condoms. The man behind the counter could not disguise his laughter." But there had been so many kinds, how could she have chosen only one? Didn't she deserve flavored? Colored? Ribbed? And the ones that promised "tickles"... She could scarcely wait.

"Poor bastard is wishing he could be in my shoes."

Graham molded her hips to his and unfastened the buttons on her braies. Jeans, actually. She loved that twenty-first-century women wore men's clothes with feminine verve, openly displaying their hips and sometimes much more. She would never be so bold to reveal as much as other women with their undergarments peeking out of their braies, but then again, she had the comfort of knowing how much Graham preferred her without any undergarments at all....

He discovered her nakedness now and it was all Linnet could do to pull away.

"But what about your celebration dinner?"

"It might have to wait. I think I might like a merry-widow celebration first."

"Wicked man."

"You haven't seen anything yet." His fingers dipped lower, urging a moan from her lips. "Remember I told you how twenty-first-century women sometimes keep toys like the Initiator around just for fun?"

"Aye." She unzipped his fly right in the middle of the kitchen, thinking microwaves left more time in life for sex and—saints preserve her—that was a very good thing.

"It occurred to me today you might get a kick out of seeing what kinds of toys are out there for your personal pleasure."

"I thought you were my personal pleasure aid?" She would never forget the way he'd made her take charge of her own pleasure—in bed and out.

"You're damn right I am. But what about the nights I work late?"

Anticipation hummed through her. "Perhaps you have a point."

Wrapping her arms around him, she indulged herself and the deep happiness she'd found.

"Who would have thought I'd fall in love with the man who once hid in my wardrobe to watch me undress?" She wriggled out of her clothes, and reached inside another bag for one of the ten boxes of different style condoms she'd purchased.

She'd wait until later to tell Graham about her high expectations.

"Who'd have thought I'd have to travel back in time nine hundred years to find the right woman?" He planted a kiss on her breast as he whipped her shirt off. "And who would have guessed she'd be so delightfully kinky?"

Linnet smiled, knowing her sexual vocabulary was coming along much quicker than other areas of knowledge.

"It is a secret all our own. You can be my hidden obsession and I'll be your personal sex goddess."

"Is that right?" He maneuvered her out of her jeans with frightening agility as he backed her against the refrigerator. "Then I'm going to start praying to the goddess for some mind-blowing sex right now."

Linnet could scarcely speak, her last conscious thought one of absolute love for Graham and the lifetime of magic ahead of them.

* * * * *

Look for the next book in the
PERFECT TIMING
miniseries
HIGHLAND FLING
by Jennifer La Brecque
coming from Harlequin Blaze
July 2006

Page-turning drama…

Exotic, glamorous locations…

Intense emotion and passionate seduction…

Sheikhs, princes and billionaire tycoons…

This summer, may we suggest:

THE SHEIKH'S DISOBEDIENT BRIDE

by Jane Porter

On sale June.

AT THE GREEK TYCOON'S BIDDING

by Cathy Williams

On sale July.

THE ITALIAN MILLIONAIRE'S VIRGIN WIFE

On sale August.

With new titles to choose from every month,
discover a world of romance in our books written
by internationally bestselling authors.

It's the ultimate in quality romance!

Available wherever Harlequin books are sold.

www.eHarlequin.com

HPGEN06

This riveting new saga begins with

by national bestselling author

JUDITH ARNOLD

The party at Hotel Marchand is in full swing when the lights suddenly go out. What does head of security Mac Jensen do first? He's torn between two jobs—protecting the guests at the hotel and keeping the woman he loves safe.

A woman to protect. A hotel to secure. And no idea who's determined to harm them.

On Sale June 2006

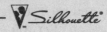

SPECIAL EDITION™

Welcome to Danbury Way— where nothing is as it seems...

Megan Schumacher has managed to maintain a low profile on Danbury Way by keeping the huge success of her graphics business a secret. But when a new client turns out to be a neighbor's sexy ex-husband, rumors of their developing romance quickly start to swirl.

THE RELUCTANT CINDERELLA

by CHRISTINE RIMMER

Available July 2006

Don't miss the first book from the Talk of the Neighborhood miniseries.